Long Path Home

Walking the South West Coast Path in Cornwall, England

Diane Winger

ISBN-13: 979-8849631226

DEDICATION

To Charlie –

My muse and favorite source of amusement.

They say that laughter keeps us young,
so that explains a lot.

ACKNOWLEDGMENTS

My longtime editor, Val Burnell, was the ideal reader for this short novel. Born and raised in England, she helped me sort out my baked beans and pasties, castles and fortresses, and advised me on avoiding having my main character come off as an Ugly American. All this, along with her usual insights to improve the story. Many thanks, Val.

I'm ever so grateful to Debby Reed for inviting me to accompany her on this grand journey which she had been planning since 2020. Her experience on other long paths led to invaluable advice on training for our trip, packing, and all the logistics. I've asked her not to give away our secrets about which parts of my story are true, partially true, or complete fabrications.

Although I hadn't heard of the book until we were well along on our adventure, I enthusiastically recommend *The Salt Path* by Raynor Winn. Her true-life account of backpacking the entire length of the South West Coast Path with her husband following a series of personal upheavals is exceptionally well-written and utterly gripping. After reading about their challenges, I'm especially thankful that Debby and I enjoyed such benign weather conditions while we pursued our far shorter trek.

I can't finish without expressing my love and gratitude to Charlie for his encouragement and willingness to see me off on my own special adventure while he romped around a different South West – Nevada, Arizona, and southern California ¬– pursuing his separate escapades. What a delight it has been to be reunited and share our stories and plan future outings, both together and separately. Forty-some-odd years together and we're still having fun.

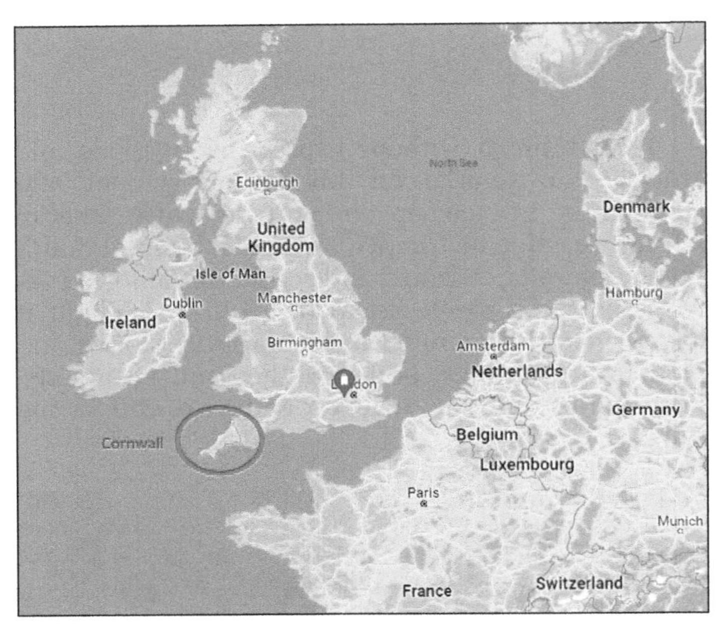

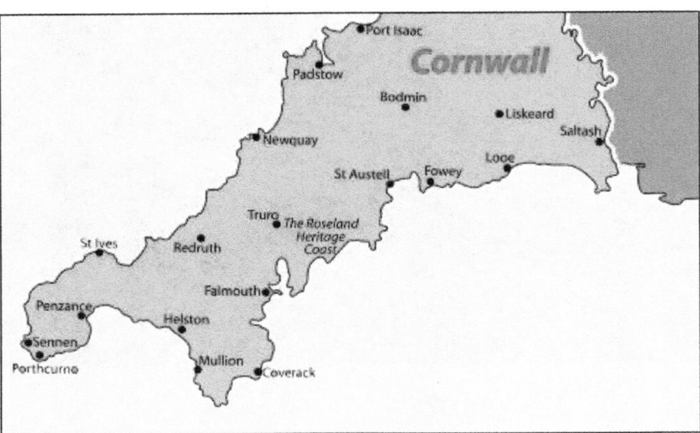

Map data ©2022 Google, GeoBasis-DE/BKG (©2009), Inst. Geogr. Nacional Europe

About this story

In April and May of 2022, I embarked on a remarkable trip to England with my long-time friend, Debby Reed, to hike over 250 miles of a portion of the South West Coast Path as it follows the serpentine coastline of Cornwall, England. As a novelist, I spent time throughout our journey imagining a fictional character, Joni, experiencing a similar odyssey but with challenges and obstacles that were totally dreamed up.

I'll admit that Joni and I share some traits. We're both short, we've both lived in Denver, and we are both enthusiastic hikers. Beyond that, Joni is a generation younger than I am and most importantly, I haven't been forced to deal with the death of a spouse. My husband, as of this writing (knock on wood), is alive and quite well, thank you very much.

Some of Joni's adventures parallel those of Debby and myself, while others are complete fabrications. At times during the story, I've scrambled locations and terrain, often because those details have already escaped my memory. While some characters were inspired by people we encountered, most are outright inventions. In other words, don't take anything in this yarn literally.

With that in mind, please join my imaginary friends for a rather long walk.

Chapter 1

"What on earth was I thinking?"

Trying to curb my increasing panic, I turn to my son in the seat beside me, but he appears to be fast asleep. I resist the urge to brush a lock of his hair back into place. He looks so much like his dad at that age, half a lifetime ago. Back when Bryan and I were newlyweds.

It was supposed to be Bryan sitting beside me on this overnight flight to London. We'd booked this bucket-list trip back in late 2019, scheduled to depart mid-spring of 2020, the spring that found us sheltering in place. That got delayed to 2021 and again the pandemic pushed back on our plans. Push came to shove, we both became ill, but I recovered while Bryan did not.

Cody, just three years out of college, lobbied for me to follow through with the trip. "You must have a friend who'd love to go hike the coast of Cornwall with you," he said. But Bryan's passing had brought home an uncomfortable truth: "our" friends were mostly "his" friends. People phoned and emailed with heart-felt condolences at first. Casseroles were delivered. A few invited me to go out for lunch or to a small gathering at their house. But after several months, the calls faded away. When I could find the energy to reach out and initiate a get-together with anyone, I struggled to identify somebody to call. Sure, I had some friends from my youth who still kept in touch, but they were scattered across the country. Meanwhile, Cody had just moved to another state for work and my empty nest felt more deserted than ever.

I realized I had never lived alone before in my entire life. From my parents' home to a college dorm to a rented house with three housemates to a shared apartment with Bryan to our first house and our second and now our third. Gathering all my nerve, I scanned the names in my contacts list, searching for friends who enjoyed hiking. Some were people we sometimes got together with for outings, while others were folks Bryan had kept in touch with from chance meetings out on trails during our travels. He was always outgoing and could easily strike up a conversation with fellow walkers, while I drafted along behind him, happy to be with such an exuberant man who made friends everywhere we went.

My list of potential travel companions wasn't very long, once I filtered out people who I couldn't imagine spending an extended period of time with, pretty much 24/7. Rose, who I knew the best of the group, was my first choice, but I learned she'd just had a knee replacement. Jenny seemed interested, but her husband wasn't and she didn't care to take a separate vacation for the three weeks I had in mind. Maggie had her own plans for that period, while Naomi was uncomfortable with the long flights involved. I even asked Melody and Stephen, despite finding him a bit overbearing. I was relieved when they declined with a vague excuse. Perhaps Stephen isn't any fonder of me than I am of him.

When I shared all this with Cody, he astonished me by suggesting that he might be able to combine his vacation and sick days and accompany me, albeit for a slightly shorter period of time. "Don't push this thing back another year, Mom. It sounds like an amazing hike. I'll go with you."

The travel company had already been paid, and my only option was to apply the funds to another trip with them – and they only operated walking excursions in Great Britain. So, why not go with a good-sized portion of our dream outing? Rather than the original 200 mile itinerary Bryan and I planned, Cody and I will shoot for 120 miles of walking along the South West Coast Path through spectacular Cornwall. I said yes to my son's suggestion, and here we are, landing in just a few more hours in London.

***

As we roll our small suitcases along the narrow street in Padstow, I feel a jolt of excitement. The big city is behind us now. Our jet-lagged brains are finished with the tasks of navigating enormous train depots and bus stations, and we're about to check into our first Bed & Breakfast before embarking on the first day of our long walk in the morning. People smile and greet us with warm hellos as we pass, taking in the quaint buildings and small harbor as we follow the GPS instructions on Cody's phone to our lodging, rooms above a traditional pub. Flower boxes adorn the upper windows and shops hug the edges of the road which can barely accommodate a single car. If one comes along as we stand in front of the pub's door, we'll probably have to step inside to allow it to pass.

"Cheers!" A young woman welcomes us as we step inside the dimly-lit room. It's exactly what I've envisioned as a classic British pub. Low ceiling with exposed dark-wood beams, a long wooden bar with a selection of beers on tap and mugs dangling overhead, rows of liquor bottles along the wall, and a stone fireplace topped with a huge blackboard announcing the surprisingly varied menu available. "Sit anywhere you like and come on up to the bar when you're ready to order."

"Oh, actually we're here to check in to our room," I say, smiling as I watch Cody scanning the draft beer selections.

"Ah, of course. You must be Joni Walker."

"Yes, and this is my son, Cody."

She grins. "And you two are walking The Path, right? How fitting! The Walkers are walkers."

"We hope we can live up to our name. Tomorrow will be our first day on the trail and I must admit I'm a bit anxious about my ability to hike over one hundred miles between now and May 3rd."

"I'm sure you'll do fine. You both look quite fit. But enough of my chattering – I'm sure you'd like to relax and perhaps enjoy a cuppa tea? Let me show you to your room."

We follow her back onto the street to the next door over from the pub entrance, where she leads us up a steep flight of stairs. Seeing how I'm struggling to lug my suitcase while grasping the bannister and trying to keep my balance on the precarious narrow steps, Cody takes it from me. "Are you sure...?" I stage-whisper at him. "I'm good," he answers, turning sideways to continue up behind me, since the stairwell is too narrow to accommodate a direct climb with luggage in both hands.

"Here we are," our hostess says after inserting a classic long metal key into the sort of door lock I've only seen in old movies. She steps aside and gestures for us to enter our room, which is a good thing since it would have been challenging to fit all three inside at the same time. The term "cozy" is quite appropriate. There are two twin beds topped with fluffy duvets, but they are pressed together to allow just enough room for two guests to be able to walk on each side. A small dresser sits beside the door to our attached bathroom, and holds an electric kettle, a bowl with tea bags, two teacups, and two wrapped packages containing shortbread cookies – or biscuits as they're referred to here. She hands me a heavy keychain holding both our room key and a key to the outside entrance. "Breakfast is in the pub starting at 9:00," she says. "Will you be wanting a Full English Breakfast, then?" Seeing a question on my face, she adds, "Your breakfast is included with the room, of course."

"Sure," I say, my exhaustion fogging my brain. "That will be fine."

I vaguely remember reading about a Full English Breakfast in the guidebooks, but can't seem to retrieve any information about what it includes beyond the impression that it is a substantial meal. That's probably a good thing – we'll need a lot of energy in the days ahead.

After she departs, Cody and I spread all our belongings on the two beds and rearrange everything. Many of the items I plan to carry in my small daypack for the hikes went into my checked luggage for the flight, and vice versa. Realizing ahead of time that I might not be thinking straight at this point, I made a list in advance of what needs to be with me on the walk and what can stay in my suitcase to be shuttled to our next B&B. "Don't forget water and snacks for the hike," I say to my son as I re-pack. "And your rain gear."

"I'm on it, Mom."

"Oh," I add, running my finger down my packing list, "and toilet paper, just in case."

"Mom. Stop. How many years did you and Dad take me out hiking? And teach me about the essential things to carry in my pack? I'm good. If we forget something on the trail tomorrow, we can swap things around when we get to the next town, right?"

He's right. This is just how I get when I'm anxious – I make lists. I obsess about everything I'm doing and what everyone else is doing. Taking a long, deep breath, I focus on letting go of my worries. The physical challenge of this trip is something I can face. I've trained hard over the past several months to be ready to hike an average of ten miles per day, with a couple of rest days built into our itinerary. I didn't know how to truly prepare myself for the chill I'm feeling deep in my soul, that empty hole I experience whenever my thoughts drift to what could have, should have been. I love that my son is here to share this adventure with me, but it should be Bryan here in the room, rearranging his suitcase. We should be in a different room down the hall – a room with a single, larger bed to be shared by a couple.

That's enough, I tell myself. Focus on what is. Enjoy this trip of a lifetime and celebrate sharing with Cody. I've spent entirely enough emotional energy over this past year on what's been lost and what could have been. For the next two weeks, it's all about the present. Today. Now.

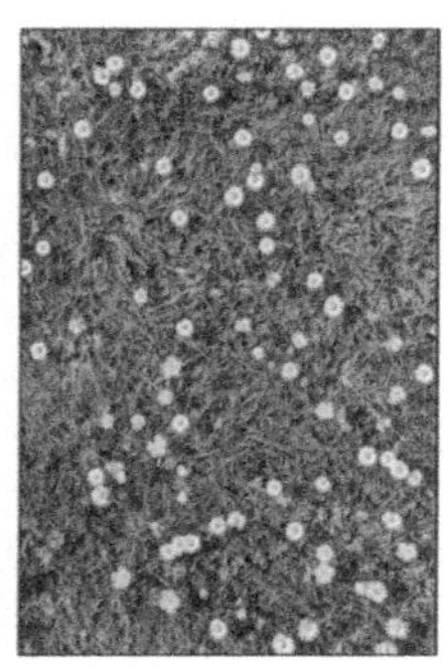

Chapter 2

I'm sure going to bed last night was far more awkward for Cody than it was for me. The last time we slept that close together was when we caved in to his pleas to let him sleep between us because there was a monster in his room. I believe he was four years old at the time. Bryan's usual sweep for monsters under Cody's bed or in his closet or behind the window blind had failed to convince him that this particular monster wasn't simply too clever to be spotted, and would surely reappear the moment his dad left the room. Coupled with our son's recent meltdown over losing his favorite stuffed toy, a tiger named Hobbs (after the comic strip), we relented and let him join us.

For this trip, I opted for pajamas rather than my usual nightgown. Cody, who I suspect normally sleeps in boxer shorts if anything at all, emerged from the bathroom wearing long PJ bottoms and a t-shirt. He crawled into bed and turned his back from the sight of his mother lying in the bed shoved close to his. "'Night, Mom."

I resisted the urge to reach over and give his shoulder an affectionate squeeze.

We each took our turn this morning changing clothes in the bathroom, and things lightened up between us once we were both dressed, our packs ready for our first day on the trail, and our suitcases ready for the luggage transport service. We head downstairs for breakfast.

A hand-written sign on the door of the pub announces, "Sorry, but we won't be open until 3:00 PM today." Surely that's just their opening time for the general public. We're lodging guests. I try the door, but it is locked.

Cody glances at his phone. "It's only five past nine. Maybe they're just running a little late for breakfast."

We peer through the windows but see no sign that anyone is inside. I try knocking. No response. We wait. Knock again. Nothing.

Suddenly we hear a disturbing caterwauling from somewhere close by. Is that a baby in great distress? No...perhaps a pair of cats screaming obscenities at each other – or courting, since that sounds the same to my ears.

"Up there," Cody says, pointing to the apex of the building across the way. Two seagulls are perched on the roof ridge, shrieking, sometimes in unison and sometimes as if in conversation. Fortunately, something convinces them to relocate to another spot a block away, but we can still hear their piercing voices.

At a quarter past nine, we decide to head over to a bakery we passed late yesterday afternoon while strolling near the harbor. Luck is with us, as the place is open for business and turns out to have a wonderful selection of breakfast options that will surely give us the energy for our first outing. After a satisfying meal, we return to the pub, which is still locked up with lights out.

"I wonder what we're supposed to do with our suitcases?" I say, frowning as I check the time on my phone.

"Oh, right! The transport company is supposed to pick them up and drive them to our next stop."

I call up our itinerary on my phone and discover a contact number for the pub. Holding my breath as my call rings through, I'm relieved when a man actually answers. I explain our situation and he advises us to bring our bags downstairs and leave them in an office room just by the foot of the stairs.

"Will the luggage people know to find them there?" I ask.

"No worries. We'll make sure this all gets sorted."

Feeling uncertain, but without an alternate plan, we fetch our bags from our room and leave them in the office.

"Are you ready?" We've donned our packs, and consulted the map we preloaded on both of our phones. Cody gives me a thumbs up. "Lead the way," I say, sliding my phone into a carrying pouch attached to the waist of my pack.

He sets out along the narrow street in front of the pub until we hit our first intersection with roads fanning out in three directions. "This one," he says, pointing to the road nearly straight ahead, but after we march about thirty paces forward, he stops. "I don't think this is right. But my location marker is jumping around, so it's hard to tell." We backtrack, then try the right-most road. I check the GPS app on my phone and we both agree that we're heading the right way now.

After following a road around the town's small harbor, we spot a wooden sign atop a post that points our way to a dirt path tunneling in amongst trees and hedges. Excited to be on our trail at last, we hike briskly, relishing the cool, clean air and the natural smells of the vegetation surrounding us. It feels so good to stretch out our legs at last after all our time riding on planes, trains, and automobiles over the past couple of days.

The trail leads us down a gentle hill to a T-intersection with another trail. I spot a square post adorned with a carved image of an acorn – the symbol our guidebooks said to watch for to guide us along our path. There's also a yellow arrow pointing up and to the left, which I interpret to mean that we need to turn left here.

We march uphill, a large grassy field to one side and a thick hedge to the other. After about ten minutes, we encounter another decision point. Do we turn right and skirt past a house, or head to our left, following another border of the field? "Uh, Mom?" Cody is frowning at his phone display. "We're really far off our track."

"How could we be? There haven't been any other places to turn." He turns his screen for me to see. "Oh. It looks like we went the wrong way back at that T-intersection."

Less than two miles into our long walk and we're lost already. Okay, so not actually lost. We just have to backtrack and try this again. When we reach the acorn and yellow arrow post again, I study it more carefully. Ah, now I see my mistake. There are different markings on each of the four sides of the square marker. I focused on the arrow intended for people arriving from a different direction than we were going.

As the day progresses, we consult our mapping software regularly to make sure we're still on course, but it soon becomes quite obvious that we continue along the route that keeps us closest to the coast. And what a coast it is! Dramatic, steep cliffs plunge off below our high vantage point, hammered by an ocean of remarkable shades of blue and green.

As we continue, pristine beaches appear far below, accessible only by water. We cross broad fields filled with wildflowers, then peer down sheer cliffs towering over rocky and jagged shores. Around each curve, a new vista appears. We hike through dense vegetation, then rise up to grassy slopes. Sometimes a small village appears around an inlet. Bryan and I had pored over images and stories about this amazing Cornwall coastline, but the reality even exceeds the most spectacular photographs. A fine mist dampens our faces, so we don our raincoats, undeterred. The moisture seems to bring out the colors of the greenery and blossoms even more. I'm enchanted.

Arriving at our next lodging, after nearly thirteen miles of walking, I feel tired but excited. The skies are clearing and the air seems to sparkle in the late afternoon sunlight. My feet ache and I'm more than ready to drop my pack and emancipate my toes from these boots. Cody wraps his arms around me and plants a noisy kiss atop my head. "This is amazing, Mom. Thanks for inviting me!"

Of course we both know that he invited himself along as a way of pushing me to go ahead with this trip. Thank goodness he did.

Chapter 3

Showing up in the breakfast room promptly at 9 A.M., we sit at one of the three tables that seems set up for breakfast. Our hostess scurries out through what I assume is the kitchen door and greets us.

"Good morning! Would you care for coffee or tea?"

Cody opts for coffee, while I ask for tea. "And white or brown bread?" she asks.

"Uh, brown?" I say and my son nods in agreement. Maybe that's whole wheat or multi-grain. We'll soon find out.

In almost no time, our table is filled with a rack of wheat toast, a mug of coffee, and a teapot for me. Then the Full English Breakfast is delivered and Cody's eyes open wide. Once our server is out of earshot, he points to his plate. "Baked beans for breakfast?"

Not only baked beans, but also a whole stewed tomato, sautéed mushrooms, hash browns, sausage, a generous slice of English bacon – not the curly bacon we eat at home – and a fried egg fill our oversized plates. "This is enough food for breakfast, lunch, and dinner," I say, spreading butter on one of the four slices of bread we've been given.

"Well, you said we need to eat plenty to keep up our energy," he says.

"If I eat all this, I don't think I'll be able to walk."

Note to self: from now on, inquire if there are any breakfast alternatives, or at least ask if they can leave off some of the items. Like the baked beans. I'm not even going to get through half of this and I hate seeing food go to waste.

Even Cody doesn't clean his entire plate, and he's like a human food vacuum that can suck down enormous quantities while remaining slim. Just like his father.

"Ready to hit the trail?" I ask when he pushes his plate away with a slight moan.

He pats his belly and grins. "Let's do it!"

We're starting to learn to read the terrain. Much of the Coast Path runs along the clifftops and wraps out around lofty headlands which jut out to sea before swinging back inland to navigate around an inlet, remaining true to the trail's theme of remaining very close to the coast. A few hours along, we encounter a warning sign across the trail, illustrated with a human figure falling off a cliff and declaring that the footpath has *foundered.* "I've heard of a horse foundering," Cody says, "but not a footpath. I thought it had to do with a messed up hoof or something like that."

I know the term has a broader meaning related to falling or failing, although I've seldom heard it used that way back home. Clearly, we should not climb around the sign to see what a foundered footpath looks like. We follow the short detour indicated instead. When it brings us back to the original trail, we look behind us and see that a sizeable chunk is missing, eaten away by the elements and tumbled to the shore hundreds of feet below.

The coastline's serpentine shape sometimes translates into a disturbingly steep descent to a narrow V where a stream flows into the ocean. Immediately after an easy step across the water, there's a strenuous ascent to the top of the cliffs again. I counted the steps the first time we encountered one of these spots – sixty-three steep, unforgiving steps in all. I refrained from counting as we reached additional arduous passageways throughout the day. Thankfully, once atop an escarpment, the terrain generally undulates over gently-rolling hills, giving our legs and knees a chance to recover. And thank goodness we're near sea level! I can't imagine tackling ascents like these on a Colorado mountain at 10 or 12 or 14,000 feet elevation!

Is it all worth it? You bet! I never dreamed that there would be so many spectacular cliff formations and gorgeous beaches and hidden coves sparkling with iridescent blues and greens. When Bryan and I pored over guidebooks and websites about hiking this route, I assumed we were seeing photos of all of the best scenery along the coast. Now I believe I could fill a coffee-table photo book with just the views we've discovered in the two days we've been walking. I refrain from focusing all my attention on taking pictures rather than fully experiencing the wonders without that distraction.

***

As usual, Cody has pulled ahead of me, so I can't actually see him when I hear his *exclamation of discontent*. That's my euphemism for his shouting a string of foul expletives.

"Are you all right, son?" I try to hurry up to reach him, but the passage ahead is a sea of dark, slimy muck.

Now he's laughing, so I slow and focus on delicately stepping on a small rock poking out of the mud, using my trekking pole for balance. Ever so carefully, I aim my other foot for a fat chunk of wood that looks like it *might* stay above the surface. Two more steps land me on more solid ground again, and I peer along the track to see Cody standing on the far side of an even wider pool of syrupy mud. The right leg of his pale beige pants appears nearly black, and he's attempting to use his hands like squeegees to wipe off some of the excess oozing dirt. Mud has splashed onto his cheek and on the tip of his nose.

"Come on across, Mom. No problem!" He laughs again and waves his hands toward me, flinging small blobs of mud in my direction.

Oh, dear. If my athletic son slipped and fell into this mire, how am I going to make it across? I take a steadying breath and set one foot on a long branch that was probably laid in the muck to help walkers work their way to the other side.

"Don't step on that one!" Cody says as I ease my other foot in the direction of a promising-looking rock. I manage to swivel slightly, changing my target to another thick branch. So far so good.

"Looking good," he says. "I think you've got this."

I plant my pole again and ease forward, but as I rotate, the tip sinks a few inches and I feel myself starting to fall. Instinctively, I step out with one foot to catch my balance and my boot squishes into the wet sludge. Before I take a tumble, I leap forward, splashing the other boot through the goo and somehow retain my footing as I arrive on the far side of the slippery mess.

"See. I knew you could do it," he says, and we both burst out laughing. He looks like he's been wallowing in mud, while I've merely been soaking my feet and the hems of my pants in a mud bath.

"You could never resist playing in a mud puddle," I say, barely able to get out the words through my chortling. "It was like you had some sort of mud radar. You could find mud during a drought. I think you figured out how to create it when you were only four or five. Remember?"

"Not really."

"Oh, yeah. You used to show up at the door covered head to toe even when you'd only have been out of our sight for a couple of minutes. I refused to let you come inside that way, so your dad would give you a 'pre-wash' under the garden hose so we could avoid clogging the bathtub drain with all that muck."

He closes his eyes a moment and grins broadly. "Now I remember. We'd pretend I was a pickup truck going through the carwash. We even had a song. *At the car wash, working at the car wash, yeah.*"

Neither of us can remember any of the rest of the lyrics, but we sing an enthusiastic, off-key rendition of the song while pantomiming washing the mud off our clothes and laughing like children. When was the last time I let loose like this? Lord, it feels good. I thought I had forgotten how.

We resume our hike, my feet squishing with each step. Thankfully, we have only another few miles to go before we can once again get out of our filthy clothes and do our best to "carwash" them first to avoid clogging up the plumbing at our next lodging. We're also thankful that the sun is now shining down on us and a warm breeze is helping to dry us out a bit. With luck, we'll be able to hand wash our hiking outfits sufficiently that we won't look terribly scuzzy when we wear them again tomorrow.

***

"What time is it?" I ask Cody, worrying over the dinner situation. When we checked in, the proprietor told us that the "Sunday Roast" meal being served in the on-site restaurant would only be available until 5:00 P.M. Rinsing off our boots and clothing took longer than I had anticipated. The flyer he gave us that describes this special feast makes it sound even more overwhelming than the Full English Breakfast.

Bring it on. I've barely eaten a thing since this morning's food orgy.

With just under ten minutes to spare, we scurry into the restaurant. Once we're seated, our waitress greets us warmly, asking if we are here for the Sunday Roast.

"Now, will you be wanting all three types of meat? We have roast beef, pork, and turkey today. You can choose any or all, and of course we serve that with stuffing, gravy, roast potatoes, carrots and parsnips, greens, cauli and cheese bake, and Yorkshire pudding."

Cody's eyes seem to glaze over. "Wow. I guess I'll try all three meats. That sounds amazing!"

"Very good. And would you care for horseradish for your beef?"

He nods, a smile filling his face. "Definitely."

"All three meats for you as well?" she asks, turning to me.

"Just turkey," I say, my mouth starting to water. I love roast turkey with gravy, but rarely have it aside from Thanksgiving.

After she departs, we both chug down water and bask in the cozy warmth of the building. Moments later, she returns with plates overflowing with hot food. "I'll be right back with the cauli and cheese," she says, then produces a small casserole dish and a large serving spoon to ladle out helpings of the steaming, gooey side dish.

"Holy cow." Cody's fork and knife hover over his plate.

"You're the one who ordered the cow. And the pig. I'm sticking with the holy turkey over here. *Bon appétit*!"

Everything tastes magnificent. I'm not sure I've ever eaten parsnips before, but assuming those are the pale-carrot-looking things, they're yummy. We eat in silence, and I find that I'm feeling quite pleased with the world.

I finish off everything except a few of the roast potatoes and the cauliflower dish. There was an interesting item on my plate that seemed a bit like a pancake baked in a muffin pan. It worked great to sop up the last of my gravy.

"I don't think I saved any room for dessert," I say, noting that Cody has cleaned his plate.

"What was that pudding called again?"

"Yorkshire pudding, I think." Too bad I'm stuffed. I've never had that dish before and I was looking forward to trying it. Maybe I can manage a little bite.

We sit and digest for a bit, and it dawns on me that several other parties have been seated since we began eating and they've been served sandwiches and other meals. So, we probably misunderstood the dinner situation here. Perhaps they stop serving the Sunday Roast special at 5:00 P.M. and go with their regular menu afterwards. That's okay. We rushed a bit to get over here in time for the special, but it was magnificent. Now fully sated, we can focus on drying the clothes we already rinsed out, washing out socks and underwear, showering, and simply relaxing for several hours.

When I see our waitress stop by a nearby table, I signal to her and she comes over.

"I think we're ready for the Yorkshire pudding now, please."

She bites her lower lip, possibly suppressing a snicker. "It looks like you both ate your puddings already, love. If you like, I can bring you another."

"We did?" Cody sounds deeply disappointed.

She scans the nearby tables, then points toward a man's plate. "There's a pudding right there. The muffin-shaped pastry?"

"Oh. That was Yorkshire pudding?"

"Yes it was, love."

"So...do you have any other desserts?" he asks.

She lists several options, and his face lights up when she mentions chocolate fudge cake. "And would you like that with ice cream or clotted cream?"

His eyebrows squeeze together, probably contemplating what clotted cream might be. I can't help him there. Yet another term for us to google when we get back to our room. "Ice cream."

Somehow I find room to manage several bites of the rich and utterly delicious concoction.

***

Our jet lag seems to be behind us as our lives begin to settle into this new pattern. Sleep. Eat. Walk. Locate our lodging, shower, eat dinner. Relax with a book – or as my son prefers, his smartphone – and go to sleep to start the cycle again.

Often, during this past year of learning to live my life without Bryan, I felt like time was my enemy. If I didn't have something specific scheduled during the day, the hours would drag on and on, and all I could think about was *how long until the noon news comes on the TV? How long until I can justify heating up a frozen dinner? How long until I can go to bed?* Everything was about killing time, yet I couldn't concentrate enough to do any work. I struggled to find ways to occupy myself between these daily "appointments," then lay awake for hours at night struggling to get my brain to stop rehashing everything about Bryan's illness, the funeral, the friends who tried in vain to help me keep busy, but gradually disappeared. I'd berate myself for not reaching out to them with an email or a phone call. For opting to go for long solo walks rather than asking a friend along.

After a number of weeks of that, I started plummeting into cycles of obsession with my work. Crunching numbers and producing charts and graphs could whisk me far away from my lonesome existence, so I'd accept a consulting gig and complete my analysis within an absurdly short timeframe. Then I'd languish for a period, incapable of focusing on the data, unable to sit at my computer. I'd spend more time anguishing over the wording of an email asking for an extension on my report delivery date than actually making progress on the task. Knowing I was recently widowed, my clients were incredibly understanding, although some simply had to look elsewhere to find a statistician to complete their project by an unmovable deadline.

Training for this trip felt like a life preserver had been thrown my way. I created a list of six nearby hikes in the foothills west of Denver and entered each one into my calendar, repeating the list for the following week. Some were short and easy, some much longer, meant to simulate being out on the South West Coast Path. On the seventh day, I did *not* rest. That was my strength day when I went to the gym and worked out on the weight machines and the free weights. If the trails were too snowy or slick, I'd wear myself out on the gym's treadmill and stair machines. After a two-hour hike or a session at the gym, I found it easier to focus once again on work, although I was careful not to take on too many consulting jobs.

Sometimes several hours would pass when I didn't think about Bryan at all. Occasionally I'd manage an entire training hike without once shedding a tear. There was starting to be a light at the end of the tunnel, and I began to entertain the remote possibility that it was *not* a train heading straight toward me.

The first morning when Cody and I began our Cornwall walk, my mind started to focus on my annoyance with the pub operators for forgetting to provide the breakfast we had paid for. After a few minutes of internal dialogues between myself and various people I wanted to imagine telling off for letting this happen, I commanded my brain to stop. Do I want to spend this trip fretting and obsessing about every little thing that doesn't go perfectly to plan, or focus on the incredible beauty around me? On the delight of sharing an experience like this with my son? I've heard the expression "live in the moment" many times. This is it – this is the moment. Stop rehashing the past, stop wishing for some future event to finally come due. I'm here. This is a magnificent experience, so don't miss it!

Cody has stopped to wait for me at a trail junction, as we'd agreed would be a smart plan since he's considerably faster than I am. He grins as I approach and presents a palm in the air for a high five. "You look like you again," he says.

Chuckling, I respond, "I would hope so. Who did I look like before? Jennifer Lawrence?"

"I wish. Well, no, not really. That would be kind of creepy." Cody's had a major crush on the actress since seeing her in The Hunger Games when he was in his teens. "No, I just mean you look more ... relaxed? Content?" He grins and my heart melts.

Smiling back, I nod. "You're right. I think I'm starting to find my way back. What about you, Cody? I've been so lost in my own feelings that I sometimes forget to check in on how you're doing." Cody and his father were very close. I've never doubted for a moment that Cody loves me, but he adored Bryan and the feeling was mutual. Cody would tell his dad anything and they loved their time together exploring the woods and scrambling up rock outcroppings in the mountains west of Denver. Some of their adventures worried me – they were far more willing to get away from the trail or scamper up loose, gravelly terrain than I ever was. But they loved discovering out-of-the-way spots that may never have been visited by other people, so I let them do their thing while enjoying staying on more established paths myself.

He pauses and considers my question seriously before answering. "I'm doing okay mostly. There are times I still miss Dad like crazy, but after all, I wasn't seeing him or talking to him daily like you were, so I think that makes it easier for me. And, you know, there's work and stuff that keeps me busy." He shrugs, and I catch an odd expression on his face for a moment. There's something else he was going to say, but stopped himself. Bryan would have known how to coax it out of him, but I know if I ask what he's thinking about, he'll assure me it's nothing.

He'll tell me in his own sweet time. Or not at all.

Chapter 4

"I'm not sure what this is telling us," I say, re-reading the comments about today's walk in the customized itinerary our British travel booking company provided us. I puzzled over it at home, then again last night, and this morning I still find it confusing.

"Apparently, we need to cross a tidal river, which might involve a ferry ride, but the ferry might not be operating yet this spring. Or we might be able to walk across a footbridge, but there are two of them and it's not clear which one is more likely to be above water. Or we could walk farther inland, or take a taxi."

I hand Cody two pages I printed out before leaving for this trip, with the confusing instructions highlighted in yellow. He frowns as he reads. "Yeah, this is confusing. So, low tide is right about now, but I'm not sure how far we are from either of the footbridges. Maybe an hour? Do you think the tide will still be low enough by then to cross?"

I shrug. I've lived my entire life in locations near the middle of a continent. What do I know about tides?

"Wait – here we go! Second page, near the bottom, it says our best option today is to use the official footbridge number one. And here are instructions for getting to it."

"Really?" He points out the pertinent instructions. "Oh. So why did they include all these details about four other crossing options if they are recommending bridge one?" Feeling my frustration level spiking over the convoluted information and my own failure to spot the final answer to my questions, I'm about to continue my tirade but manage to stop myself. Let it go. It doesn't matter now. I turn and gaze out at the ocean, reminding myself to focus on this extraordinary trip and the delight of spending so much time with my son.

Meanwhile, he's studying the map on his phone. "Okay, I see it. No problem. The GPS track we downloaded takes footbridge number one, so we just keep doing what we've been doing all along – follow that track."

Of course, there have been a few times when we've forgotten to check our maps and have headed off our track, but we've been able to rectify those mistakes easily. "Cody, lead on. Let's find our bridge and hope it isn't underwater because we got there too late."

The Coastal Path winds through town, then angles down to a beach at a slightly lower elevation. We head toward the ocean along the sandy trail. To our left, shallow pools of water and a stream running only inches deep are the only evidence that this strip of beach is sometimes filled with a tidal river. If we didn't mind getting our boots wet, we could probably just walk across to the other side, but I'm happier when we spot a boardwalk spanning the soggy expanse. It will be under water once the tide rises eight or ten inches, but it is a dry path for us at the moment, and that's all we need. No long detours for us this morning, nor trying to find some alternate mode of transportation.

How crazy that I let myself get all worked up over something that turned out to be so simple.

As we get farther from town, we return to the high cliffs. The scenery continues to mesmerize me. We spot places in the cliffs we've just traversed where the wind and water have carved out enormous caves, towering at least fifty feet in height. We cross immense fields of dense, short grasses which would be the envy of any golf groundskeeper back home. Do they grow to this perfect, uniform height, or is this the result of grazing sheep? Either way, the broad expanses of green are lovely to see and delightfully springy to walk upon.

My stomach has been growling for several minutes when we spot a pair of benches up ahead. A couple are already seated on one and appear to be enjoying a trailside picnic with a spectacular view. They smile and nod as we approach.

"Hiya," the man says when we stop. He gestures toward the empty bench. "Fancy a wee sit down?"

"Don't mind if we do," I answer, smiling.

We exchange a few pleasant remarks about the lovely view as we set our trekking poles aside and remove our packs, then begin fishing out our lunch selections. I'm sticking with an apple dipped in peanut butter, with a slice of cheese as a chaser. Cody has a packet of crackers and a small tub of hummus. Our new friends watch with interest as we lay everything out between us on the bench.

"Ever try Marmite, mate?" The man holds out a small jar clearly labeled MARMITE along with a plastic spreader.

Cody shrugs. "Not that I know of."

I've never tried it either, although I think it's something like Vegemite down in Australia. And all I know about Vegemite is to sing along to the song, "Down Under," where it goes, "He just smiled and gave me a Vegemite sandwich." So I know you can enjoy it on bread.

"Just spread a wee bit on a cracker and give it a go," the woman explains.

My son dips the knife in the jar and slathers the dark-colored substance on one of his crackers. The lady's eyes widen as he takes a generous bite. Clamping his hand over his mouth, his eyes scan wildly, but he hangs in there, chewing and swallowing the food. "Oh my god!" he mutters through his hand, grasping for his water bottle then swigging down half its contents. The British folks are clearly trying their best not to laugh.

"Are you going to be all right, love?" the woman asks. "I've never seen anyone put nearly that much on their cracker before."

Cody coughs and nods, then drinks more water. His face is returning to a normal color after turning quite purple. "That was really salty," he manages. "And...I don't think I've ever tasted anything like that before. What is it?"

"It comes from brewer's yeast. Very good for you."

"Right. Wanna try some, Mom?" he says, holding the coated cracker out to me.

I told myself before this trip that I would be sure to order traditional British dishes, but was thinking of Fish and Chips or Cornish Pasties. I hadn't considered Marmite. "Only if I can tone it down. Do you have another cracker?" He hands one to me and I dab the knife into the thick layer of Marmite on Cody's wafer, then spread the miniscule bit over the fresh cracker.

"It's...different," I say after taking the smallest bite I can manage. Winking at my son, I finish off the rest of my portion and smile. "I might be able to get used to the taste."

"Good on you!" the man declares as we hand him back his jar. "I'm Roger and this is my wife Nell. Are you from the U.S. or is it Canada?"

"The U.S. I'm Joni and this is my son Cody," I reply. "I assume you are both British?"

Nell says, "That we are. We're from the London area and we've been walking sections of The Path for six years now. When we reach Perranporth, we'll have completed all 630 miles!" As I've noticed several times already, when people refer to "The Path," the emphasis on Path makes it clear that they mean this South West Coast Path, and no other. I'm sure they capitalize it in their heads. That reminds me of how hikers and climbers around the Denver area will talk about "heading up to the Park," and that's understood to mean Rocky Mountain National Park rather than any city park or other National Park in Colorado.

"Wow, 630 miles!" we say in unison. I glance at my son and add, "Maybe we'll have to keep coming back for the next five years and finish the entire walk." He looks a bit alarmed at this until I wink to let him know I'm just pulling his leg.

Roger and Nell pack up and wish us well as they take off for their final stop. "Thanks for the Marmite," Cody calls after them and that elicits laughter and another wave goodbye.

"Everyone seems so nice and upbeat," I say. "I can't think of any people we've passed along the trail who haven't said hi and smiled at us."

"Even the dogs seem laid back."

True. I tend to be a bit nervous when a strange dog runs toward me on a trail, unleashed and with their owner far behind. But the dogs we've encountered – and there have been quite a few – have all trotted past with barely a glance our way, and their people have struck me as calm and friendly.

Finished with our snacks and with the salty taste of Marmite washed away by our more familiar foods, we set off again, enjoying thinking of nothing but the trail ahead of us, the ocean to our right, and the meditative tranquility of having nothing to accomplish today but to walk.

As we approach our destination, we find ourselves crossing a broad beach. Our map indicates that we can find an exit to lead us to the town of Perranporth, but we fail to find an obvious way to climb up the sandy hills leading away from the water.

"Maybe up this ramp," Cody says, checking his phone before quick-stepping up a steep section of sand that turns into a narrow passageway through the dunes. I follow, relieved to hit slightly firmer sand that doesn't shift so much beneath my feet. The natural corridor rises gradually, eventually opening up to a vista of sand dunes surrounding us. There is evidence of footprints in many directions, so we consult our tracking maps again.

Cody points. "That way, I think." We weave our way among the hills of sand until we hit a spot where our only option is to climb up one of the dunes. He chooses one that will take us a bit higher and farther from the beach and I follow.

"Um – I don't think that was the right way."

We've crested the dune and there's no obvious trail anywhere nearby. The good news is that we can see more of the terrain around us, but the bad news is that all we see are dunes and more dunes.

"I think we need to head further inland," I say. "This sand can't go on forever, and once we get out of it, we'll be able to see where we are and maybe just walk along a road into town." Because I can see on my map that there is a road paralleling the ocean, and it isn't terribly far away.

We descend and attempt to wind our way in the direction of the road, but we're forced to scramble up yet another dune. As I huff my way up, silently cursing the shifting sands beneath my feet, I hope we'll be able to spot the road once we reach the top.

No such luck. "Mom, look! A runner!"

The bare-chested man is moving along at a good clip back near where we emerged from our original passageway. Clearly he knows how to get out of this dune maze. We scurry back down and miraculously find our way to a spot where we can call out to him before he disappears.

"How do we get out of here?" I shout, plunge-stepping my way down the shifting slopes in his direction.

He waits up for us and points back the way he came. Now that we're standing beside him, we can clearly see the more obvious path heading where we are trying to go. We thank him as he takes off running again, and this time manage to follow the relatively flat route until we start seeing more and more people, trail signs, and a well-trodden path to follow to the nearest road.

When we first stepped onto that vast beach, I had figured we'd be at our lodging within twenty minutes, based on the distance I measured on the map. It took us over an hour, but hey – we had an adventure, didn't we!

Chapter 5

Two ghost ships appear on the horizon. Of course they're nothing so mysterious as that – simply a pair of rock formations jutting out of the ocean. But with the thin fog clouding our view to sea, it's easy to let our minds wander and imagine great tales of ancient sea vessels sailing through the eons only to reappear in our modern world, their long-dead crews gazing to shore, longing to finally, finally make land.

At least that's the *Twilight Zone* tale that Cody and I concocted as we strode along our route this morning. Other, more recent ghosts may be going about their business at the various ruins of old tin mining operations we encounter along the coast. We can only guess at their history, since none of the structures is graced with signs explaining their purpose or era. I guess we should have perused the guidebooks again last night.

The terrain varies widely, taking us from broad, treeless slopes out to bluffs overlooking spectacular, rocky coves. Remembering the highlighted features listed in our itinerary for today, we pull out binoculars to survey the rocks jutting out of the ocean and delight in spotting seals basking in the sun.

We have a long day of walking planned. Scanning the views ahead of us, we count several spits of land jutting away from the mainland, and we try to guess how many of them we'll visit this afternoon before eventually reaching today's destination.

What we can never spot before drawing close are the inlets and coves. Will the Coast Path offer a kind and gentle slope down to a beach, or will we be dropped a few hundred feet to a narrow crossing, then be faced with a towering ascent back to our previous heights? Do the Brits not know about building switchback trails to zig-zag at a reasonable grade up and down hills? If they know about them, they've chosen to ignore the concept.

Let's build a trail of steps. Exceptionally steep steps.

Thank goodness I have a hiking pole! I'd be terrified of pitching forward as I take a series of huge steps downward if I didn't have it for stability. And I'd literally have to crawl up the steps without the pole to help me heave myself from one to the next, often located at knee height or higher. The long stickers in the lovely gorse bushes quickly cured me of imagining that grasping the vegetation that hugged the narrow stairways would be at all helpful.

Cody, with much longer legs than mine, seems to fare slightly better, although at 5 foot 8 (with shoes on), he's not exactly tall. He's lean and leggy, though, built like his dad. In his teens, he used to run the same trails in the foothills west of Denver that I used for my training hikes. I'm not sure how he got ready for this trip, though, since any hiking paths around Dallas are mainly flat. And hot, even during the springtime.

It isn't pretty, but I survive a double-header – two sets of extra tall steps at the very end of today's trek. But pity the poor man we passed going in the opposite direction. As we reached the top of one of the knee-busting, near vertical sections, two young men around Cody's age toting full backpacks struggled up toward us, so we waited to let them reach flatter ground. Seeing nobody else below them, I started down, but soon spotted a man I'd gauge to be slightly older than I am – perhaps late fifties or so – staggering up the steps. His backpack looked enormous on him, despite being a rather substantially-sized man himself. No hiking pole. I moved aside, watching as he'd somehow lurch upward another step, then teeter in exhaustion before tackling the next rise. I was terrified that he might lose his balance and have that monstrous pack yank him over backwards where he'd tumble down the steep incline with no means of stopping his plunge. "Almost to the top," I said as he struggled up to where I stood, his face purple and dripping sweat. I think he gasped out *Thanks*, but it was difficult to tell. Poor man. I hope he and his younger companions arrived at their campsite soon, before he collapsed on the trail!

When we arrive at our cozy hotel, I groan when I spot the steep, narrow staircase leading up to our room, picturing myself struggling like that man with the oversized load, then gratefully accept Cody's offer to lug my bag upstairs. Immediately after closing our door, we both yank off our boots and collapse onto the beds.

"Man, my legs are like spaghetti and my feet ache," he moans. "Why did all those frickin' steps have to be at the end of our day?"

So it isn't just me.

***

When we return to our room after an excellent dinner in a bright and modern restaurant virtually next door to our lodging, Cody is immediately engrossed with something on his phone. I putter around a bit, laying out my alternate hiking shirt and preparing my pack for tomorrow, checking to see if the clothes I rinsed out in the sink and laid on the radiator are dry yet. He's been muttering under his breath and his thumbs are flying over the virtual keyboard on his phone.

"What's going on over there? Are you writing the next great American novel?" I try to keep my tone light, hoping he won't find my question too intrusive. After all, he's not a child anymore, and I've tried to keep that fact in the forefront of my mind when I've wanted to know what is going on in his life. If he was still fifteen, I'd have the right – as his mother – to know who he was hanging out with and where he spent his time. I would still love to learn every detail, but he's a twenty-five-year-old man now, so he can share whatever he wishes and hold back anything he likes.

He raises his hand, signaling *just a moment*, then completes whatever he's been typing. With a sigh, he sets his phone on the bed and looks over at me.

"So..." He pauses. I keep my mouth shut. While it's not at all unusual for him to start a new topic with *so*, I know this long pause means he's about to tell me something I may not be thrilled about. Like when he borrowed the car soon after he got his license. *So...I kind of backed into a light pole and dented the bumper.* Or when he decided to drop his Physics major in college and go with Computer Information Systems. He thought Bryan wanted him to follow in his footsteps, but we both just wanted Cody to study whatever was his own passion.

Meanwhile, my son is still rehearsing whatever it is he needs to tell me. This is the longest gap between *so* and the rest of the story I've ever experienced from him, and it's making me extremely apprehensive.

"So...?" I prompt.

"So, I have good news." It sounds more like a question than a statement, but I nod encouragingly. "I was waiting to tell you until I knew it was a sure thing, but now it is, so...I've got a new job!" His face glows with enthusiasm. "You know I really wanted to focus on AI, but couldn't find any openings when I graduated."

Artificial Intelligence was his primary focus during college, although he was required to take a broad range of courses related to computers – coding, user interfaces, numerical analysis, and more. "And now you'll be working on AI projects?" I ask.

"Yeah. This is like breakthrough stuff they're working on. I just heard about the job opening about a week before we were heading over here, and had a remote interview where I could tell they were super interested in me."

"That's wonderful, son. I assume that's what all your texting or emailing has been about tonight."

"Right." He looks away from me and I sense there may be a bad news part of what he's got to say. "So..."

And here we go again. I gesture for him to continue.

"So, the other good news is that they're located in Boulder."

"You're moving back home?!" Nothing else he may say can dampen my joy at the thought that my only child will be living nearby again. It was so hard to see him move off to Dallas for work. I know he's missed the mountains and experiencing all four seasons. While he's seemed comfortable with his job as a programmer, I've never sensed that he loved his work.

He looks anxious. "I'm not sure exactly how that'll work. There's no way I can afford to live in

Boulder without sharing a house again with several people, and I'm not exactly crazy about that idea. But I'll only need to go into the office about twice a month, so I could live anywhere in metro Denver or further north of Boulder where I could make that drive, but mostly work from home."

"That sounds like you'll be able to figure something out. When do you start? Have you given notice at your current job? Do you think you'll move back to Colorado right away, or do you have much time left on your apartment lease?"

"Whoa, Mom! Yes, I've given notice at work and to my landlord. Everything's cool there. But I kind of messed up and I've been trying to fix it but I don't think I can without losing out on the new job and I'm really, really sorry."

He looks almost despondent, but he's totally lost me. "Honey, whatever it is, maybe we can fix it if we put our heads together. Tell me what you're talking about."

He braces with a deep breath. "They offered me the job and said they wanted me to start on Monday, the 2nd."

"Of June?"

"No. The 2nd of May."

"But we don't fly home until May 6th."

"Yeah," he sighs. "I guess I was so excited to land my dream job that I got confused about the date. I was thinking that was the Monday *after* we got back. But they sent me an email today with all sorts of stuff about coming in this *coming* Monday and I went back through our messages and that's what they were saying all along. Not May 9th – May 2nd. I messed up."

I huff, waving off his concerns. "Surely they'll understand that you're in England and they can just push back your start date by a week."

"You don't understand, Mom. One of the things they focused on big-time during my interviews was how they need someone who they can rely on to meet deadlines. They're often competing for contracts with medical researchers who need a solution ASAP. How is it going to look if I can't even read a frickin' calendar to know when I'm supposed to show up for work? I wasn't the only qualified candidate for this position. If I ask for a delay, they're just going to pass me by for someone they can rely on."

I'm about to tell him that a company which is that rigid with a new employee is likely to ask him to give up far more personal time than is reasonable. Maybe they aren't worth working for. But I see the longing in his face. The joy when he describes his new position. And I would absolutely love, love, *love* for him to be living closer to me again.

"You want to fly back early."

He nods. "Mom, I'm so sorry. I know I committed to doing two weeks with you, but I don't know if I'll ever get this great an opportunity again." He bites his lip and I can see the little boy who just knocked over a lamp while throwing his ball in the house – something he knew he wasn't supposed to do. "Are you pissed at me?" he mumbles.

"Of course not." I cross the room and spread my arms wide and he wraps himself around me for a long hug. "It'll be okay. We can change our flights. I guess we'll have to figure out where the train stations are in relation to our next stop or two and..."

"Wait. You don't need to go back early because of me. You've been wanting to take this trip for years, Mom. Don't cut it short. I've already got my transportation figured out. I'll still walk with you to St. Ives and stay the first night there. I can leave early the next morning and you can still enjoy your rest day and hike on to Penzance the following week."

Continue on alone? *Alone?* I've become far too familiar with what that experience feels like. Even with Cody here on this trip, I've been struggling to shut off my mind when it has tried to remind me that my dream had been to share this remarkable experience with Bryan. And that I'll be alone again when I return home.

Shaking my head, I protest, but he holds me by my shoulders and looks me straight in the eye. "Mom, you *need* to finish this hike. Think about how strong you've proven to be – not just physically but your determination. Remember when I told you that you look like yourself again?"

I manage a weak smile and nod. Look at us. The child has become the teacher, the cheerleader, the supporter. We've swapped places.

"I don't know if it's because of the fifty miles we've walked and all those stinking steps we've conquered or if it's because we're in a magical place where our whole world has become ocean and cliffs and beaches and baked beans at breakfast. Or maybe it's because time keeps passing since Dad left us, and we're learning to live without him. Whatever the reason, you've changed. You're stronger than I ever realized you were. I'm really proud of you, Mom."

Wiping away a tear, I reach up and hold his face in both hands. "How did I get to be so lucky to have such a wonderful son as you?"

"I had great parents who raised me right," he says, blinking rapidly.

We gaze at each other for some time before we're ready to release each other. "I need a little time to think about what I want to do," I tell him. Even with his pep talk, there's a small voice telling me I'll feel lost and unhappy if I continue on the Coast Path by myself. Yet...I do feel stronger than before. Think of how I might feel if I continue on for another fifty miles! On my own.

Photo credit: Debby Reed

Chapter 6

Today dawned clear and bright and beautiful. Unable to make up my mind about leaving early with Cody or sticking it out for the second half of the trip on my own, I promise myself to come to a decision before we reach our lodging in Hayle today. Only two more days of walking if we return to the U.S. together. *Two*. That sounds so short, so abrupt an end to this journey. But if I stay, I'm facing an entire week completely on my own. No one to consult the map when I come across a confusing junction of trails. No one to share a meal with and talk about our favorite parts of the day and a thousand other topics. No one to help navigate the trains and Heathrow airport when it's time to return home.

I shove those thoughts to the background and do my best to clear my mind and simply focus on the walk. I have hours to go before I make my decision, and I want to enjoy this day as much as I can.

Our path takes us out to a headland where a nearby island holds a lovely lighthouse and frisky seals hanging out on the rocks and within small coves visible below our vantage point. Some are close enough that we can pick them out with the naked eye, but of course our binoculars bring them into clearer focus. We've stopped here for a trail-side lunch break, as have several other hikers, although there's plenty of room for everyone to spread out nicely.

Wanting to vary my food selection, I bought a tin of sardines at a small shop yesterday, thinking they'd be tasty with the cracked pepper crackers I also picked up. Cody scrunches up his face when I open the container and insists that I move well away from him to eat my odoriferous meal. Although I try my best to avoid spilling anything, by the time I finish eating, there are blobs of sardine-infused tomato sauce scattered around me on the native vegetation. Feeling guilty for having been sloppy, I consider how to clean up the droppings, but realize the two seagulls who have landed nearby are eyeing the mess eagerly. Since we've observed these bold birds enthusiastically eating from garbage cans or gobbling down dead fish and animal droppings, I'm pretty sure this spot will look pristine moments after I depart. I wrap the stinky can tightly in a plastic bag and stash it carefully in the top flap of my pack. What a mess. I'll stick with apples, cheese, and peanut butter from now on.

As we approach civilization, we pause to admire a group of wild ponies enjoying a long drink at a trough, separated from admiring tourists by a single wire on a fence line. Beautiful little animals, with thick, rich coats, but probably not all that wild compared to the wild horses that roam some areas of the American west. I take a photo, then step back where I can observe my son admiring the lovely creatures. Spending this week with him, sharing such a remarkable journey, has been a healing experience – I think for both of us. He pulls his phone from a holder on his pack, steps away from the ponies, and his focus turns away from his surroundings. We're near enough to a town to have coverage again, and it's clear that he's already back home mentally, thinking about his new job and finding a place to live near Boulder.

I've made up my mind. I'm not ready for this special experience to end. With Cody's career move, I'll be able to see him on a regular basis again, so this is no longer a rare opportunity to enjoy my son's company.

As for going it alone – isn't that what I've been doing this past year? The important difference is that I'm starting to realize that I *can* do this. I'm stronger than I ever dreamed I could be – physically and emotionally. I. Can. Do. This.

***

We seem to have programmed the wrong address for our hotel into our GPS maps. Actually, I'm surprised the software has done so well up until now, since they don't appear to use actual street numbers in many of these small villages. It seems that locals know buildings by their names – William's Cottage, Cliff House, Tin Miner B&B, Cornwall Hotel, Queen's Arms, King's Arms. Cody, who seems more anxious than usual to find our place and get settled in, approaches a young man around his age and asks for directions. "Just on the next street, mate," he says, pointing the way. "Turn right. It's a yellow building with a blue sign over the door."

We head that way. Turning the corner as instructed, we spot the hotel easily and march toward it until Cody stops abruptly and I nearly walk into him. I look down the road and spot a mountain of a man marching swiftly in our direction. He's dressed in a muscle shirt and knee-length shorts and has the physique to justify his light clothing. With a drooping mustache and a red bandana tied around his head, tattoos decorating the enormous muscles on his arms and exposed upper chest, and a swaggering strut, my mind goes immediately to *motorcycle gang leader* or *bouncer at a bar in a rough neighborhood.* He halts directly in front of the yellow building with the blue sign.

"Should we walk on past?" I hiss to my son, hoping my voice doesn't carry to the scary man. I glance his way and see that he has plastered a smile on his face that looks almost like a grimace. Cody forges ahead, while I follow nervously. I think he's going for the *Hey, I'm just a friendly little guy. Please don't hurt me* approach.

"Hey, there," Cody says in as bright a tone as he can manage. I hear a hint of a tremor in his voice, but he advances right over to the giant. "How's it goin'?"

Muscle-man's face transforms with a genuine smile. "Going great! If you're looking for The Blacksmith Hotel, you've found it," he says, tilting his head toward the entrance.

"Uh, yeah. We are."

"Great! My wife and I are staying here tonight as well. Looks like you folks are walking the South West Coast Path, too."

I realize that I've been staring at him in amazement. He sounds American, as I had guessed by his appearance. But I was expecting a loud, gravelly bass voice, perhaps a growling tone. Instead, his delivery is gentle and warm. He'd be perfect as a radio announcer for a late night smooth jazz station. From a distance, I thought he was scowling, but now I think that was an illusion caused by his long mustache. He reaches out an enormous paw to shake my hand. "Nice to meet you. I'm Larry," he says as his hand totally engulfs mine. His grip is remarkably gentle, and an image of him tenderly cupping a tiny kitten in his hand flashes through my mind.

"Joni," I say. "And this is my son, Cody."

They shake as well. “Hey, here I am gabbing away when I’m sure you two are ready to settle into your room, dump your packs, and pull off your boots. Here, let me get the door.”

Larry turns us over to our hotel host, Malcolm, and heads upstairs. “Maybe we’ll see each other at breakfast in the morning. Have a great evening, Joni. Cody. Pleasure to meet both of you.”

Malcolm insists on carrying my suitcase up to our room and as soon as he departs, we do exactly what Larry predicted – drop our packs, yank off our boots, and plop onto our beds.

“Larry seems like a nice guy. Not what I expected,” Cody says as he wiggles his toes.

“Same here, I’m embarrassed to admit. I was quick to pre-judge him. I didn’t expect him to be so soft-spoken and friendly.”

“Yeah, right?”

Chapter 7

At breakfast, I'm surprised when Malcolm delivers a chocolate croissant with a single candle to my spot. Cody must have told him it's my birthday. He, Cody, and the other guests join in on singing as I blow out the flame.

"Thanks, son," I say softly.

"Yeah, well, I know you guys planned this walk to celebrate your 50th, Mom, and I'm sorry that didn't turn out. But I wanted you to have something special for your 52nd birthday. I know it's not much, but..."

"It means a lot, Cody." I blink rapidly, then push the sadness aside. Been there, done that. I smile broadly as I take a bite of my birthday treat. "Oh, yum!" I moan. "Malcolm, this is delicious!"

We enjoy a delightful conversation with Larry, again dressed in a muscle shirt and shorts, and his wife Eileen, a trim and fit lady with a long blond-turning-to-gray braid down her back and a tie-dyed tank top. Without his bandana, Larry appears older and is nearly bald. They tell me that their oldest daughter recently married, the middle girl is in Peru as a Peace Corps volunteer, and their youngest is wrapping up her first year of college, with no plans to return home for the summer.

"Empty-nesters, huh? I know that feeling," I say, offering a wink in my son's direction.

Eileen grins. "We figured this would be an ideal time for both of us to take a sabbatical and travel." It turns out that she's a history professor at their local community college in South Dakota while he's been working for the past fifteen years in a program for troubled youth.

"We're thinking of moving on to something different," Larry explains. "Something less stressful for me. Eileen qualifies for retirement in five more years, so that would be an ideal time for a change. We'd love to work as camp hosts, maybe with two locations that let us do both summer and winter."

I raise an eyebrow. While living in a campground in a lovely setting sounds appealing, I can't imagine being the people who have to deal with unruly guests, trashed-out restrooms, and various emergencies that may crop up any time, day or night.

He continues, "We're not averse to hard work, and I think I'm adept at handling people in nearly any situation."

She adds, "Larry may look pretty darn scary to folks, but he's actually a very gentle person who can usually calm folks down." She smiles warmly at him across the table.

That sums up my impression of the man quite well.

Cody and I are ready to hit the trail before the other couple, but we exchange hopes that our paths cross again out there on the Coast Path. Not long after we wind our way out of town, the trail slips between an old cemetery and a small, stone church. We wander among the grave markers, the land now carpeted in wildflowers, reading the inscriptions and challenging each other to find the oldest of the gravestones. I gravitate to the markers shaped as Celtic crosses and the one-inch-thick slabs poking out of the ground, which I suspect are the oldest. Unfortunately, any inscriptions they once held have been polished away by centuries of wind and rain. Cody wins our contest with a stone dated 1793, but I'm unable to make out the last digit.

Our relatively short walk today – less than eight miles! – brings us into the charming town of St. Ives, filled with a plethora of tourists exploring the waterfront area. It's a bit shocking, yet fun, to encounter crowds of people again after all our solitude on the trail and the quiet of the smaller villages we've been staying in. The South West Coast Path is routed right through town on attractive and popular paved walkways with views of the ocean as well as numerous hotels and private homes close to shore. Civilization.

We work our way up steep streets leading us inland several blocks where we locate our lodging, a B&B that was probably once a large single family home. Unsure if we'll be allowed to check in this early, we're pleased when the owner, who we learn goes by Penelope, spots us hovering on the front walk and invites us inside – but only after we've removed our boots, if you please.

Standing inside the entry, boots in hand, packs on backs, we listen as she regales us with a commentary on American politics – she hates Republicans and Democrats alike – and the state of the world – a bloody mess. She transitions seamlessly to a lengthy lesson about the history of St. Ives, which I might have enjoyed much more if my stomach weren't growling and my stocking feet weren't starting to ache from standing on the hardwood floor. I stare with anticipation at our two suitcases sitting at the foot of the stairs to the second floor, longing to grab mine and head up to our room.

Penelope segues to a description of what we will be encountering on the next part of our journey along the Coast Path. "It starts out just as lovely as can be," she says, "but then you'll come to an area filled with enormous boulders where you must take giant steps to climb up. You may manage them," she says, pointing at Cody, "but with your short legs," she says to me, "I'm not sure what you'll be able to do!" She demonstrates with an awkward lunge past three of the steps on the staircase. No worries, then. I know about those obscenely tall steps along The Path.

I smile. "I imagine I'll work it out. I do a fair amount of hiking back home in the mountains of Colorado. And we've hiked over seventy miles already, coming from Padstow. "

She shakes her head. "I walked this next part and had to claw at the rocks for any sort of purchase! My hands were covered in dirt. There was even dirt under all my fingernails!" She waves her hands like claws high in the air to emphasize her point.

"I'll give my mom a hand if she needs it," Cody says. I don't correct him to explain that I'll be tackling that section alone, since he's leaving in the morning. A comment like that could lead to another ten minute dissertation from Penelope on any number of topics.

"We're pretty famished and would really like to head back to the harbor for lunch," I say turning toward the staircase.

Our hostess launches into a review of about a dozen possible lunch stops. Unable to stand it any longer, I interrupt her, asking if we can take our things to our room now, or if the room isn't ready, can we simply leave our backpacks with our bags and return later?

"Oh. Yes, of course your room is ready. Right up this way."

Penelope shows us to our room upstairs and I claim that we need to change clothes as I smile and very gradually ease the door closed as she continues babbling. "Thank you so much." I say, smiling broadly. "See you tomorrow at breakfast, then. Bye now," I add with a little *goodbye* wiggle of my fingers just before gently latching the door closed.

Cody is half curled up on his bed, trying to suppress his laughter. "Way to go, Mom! You've turned into a badass!" he says in a stage-whisper, then has to bury his face in the pillow to keep from laughing out loud.

Nobody has ever described me as badass before, or anything remotely similar. Never tough nor a fighter. Yet, I handled that pretty darn well. As well as Bryan might have, although he may have taken an even more direct tack. *Badass*. I think I like it.

We change into our clean(er) clothes and sneakers, then return down the steep streets to the harbor area which is filled with narrow roads lined with pubs and bistros and restaurants and gift shops. Spotting an attractive seafood place right beside the shore, we are thrilled when we're offered a table on their partially-covered patio overlooking the beach. I order a plate of mussels while Cody opts for a shrimp dish. We add a side of bread described as *seeded wholemeal*, which turns out to be utterly delicious, especially when slathered with sweet butter. Both of our seafood dishes are exquisite and generous. Sated, we end up taking half the bread with us for later.

Cody leaves tomorrow morning. I savor our time together as we explore the shops and watch the boats in the harbor. We'd noticed a jumble of stones just below the sidewalk leading beside the shore, where someone had carefully created impossibly-balanced rock cairns. One stone, diamond-shaped and roughly a foot tall, was perched on a point atop a tiny glass bottle, which in turn was set on a rounded rock. As we reverse our route and walk past that area again, there's a man down there attempting to balance an even larger, angular rock on the point of one poking up out of the piles of stones.

"No way," Cody whispers, as if even the air movement from his voice might topple the upper rock from our position ten feet away.

The Rock Whisperer lifts his hands away in slow motion and the sculpture remains in place. We hear applause and realize that others have gathered at the railing above the rocks to watch his delicate work. When we return again several hours later, in search of a light evening meal, the tide has come in and the rock art gallery is under water, undoubtedly rearranged by the power of the ocean.

Having had such a huge meal at lunchtime, we figure this evening is an ideal time to try a local specialty we've been seeing advertised in every village we've passed through – a Cornish pasty. Arriving just before it closes, we hurry into an attractive bakery with signs on the street declaring their version as the most authentic in all of Cornwall.

The half-moon shaped baked goodies are featured prominently in their display case, with choices of traditional beef, chicken, or vegetarian fillings.

"They look like apple turnovers," Cody says. "But they aren't sweet?"

"I don't think so. Not with steak and potato filling. More like a beef pot pie, but not so messy."

An attractive young lady approaches us at the counter. "Hello. What would you like?"

Remembering a phrase in one of my guidebooks, I reply, "We'd like to try a *proper* Cornish pasty and it seems like we're in the right place for that."

I can tell she's trying not to laugh at me, so I grin to let her know that I realize my emphasis on *proper* was justifiably humorous, given my obvious American accent. I glance over at Cody and he's gazing at the woman with puppy-dog eyes. As I noted, she's quite pretty.

With a smile, she asks, "Which flavor *pasty* would you care for?" and I realize what has amused her. I pronounced it like *pastry*, but without the 'r'. PASTE-ee. She called it a PASS-tee. Pass me a pasty.

Demonstrating that I was paying attention, I request a chicken pasty – PASS-tee – but don't go so far as to say, "Pass me a chicken pasty." Cody chooses beef. We take our treats outside and find a picnic table overlooking the water. Realizing we didn't ask for any flatware, and that he might have another opportunity to be in close proximity to the lovely young woman who waited on us, Cody scurries back to the bakery, but it's closed for the evening.

"I think we can manage these like finger food," I say when he returns. "I was reading that pasties were the meal of choice for miners who needed something they could easily pack away and eat down in the tin mines during work breaks."

"Kind of like a robust, self-contained sandwich." He picks his up, partially wrapped in paper, and takes a bite out of the end. "Tasty."

"Shouldn't that be TASS-tee?" He chuckles, shaking his head. We enjoy our light dinners and Cody bemoans the fact that we hadn't tried pasties earlier in the week. "These would make a great lunch on the trail. I wonder if they'll be open early enough in the morning for me to get some for my train trip to London."

I bite my lip and struggle to put on a brave face. Once I see him off in the morning, I'm going solo. Thankfully, we were already scheduled to spend two nights here in St. Ives, with tomorrow our first designated rest day. Frankly, I feel ready to move on to our – no, make that *my* next stop along the Coast Path. When Bryan and I planned out this itinerary, I was sure I'd be exhausted and sore and ready to take a break at this point. Remarkably, it feels odd to do anything other than hitting the trail each morning. It's going to feel even odder to head out without Cody.

But what the heck – I'm a badass, right? If I keep telling myself that, I'll be fine. Still, I am feeling apprehensive about the boulder-clawing section of trail described by our talkative hostess.

***

The train station is close to the place where we enjoyed our delicious lunch yesterday. Rolling a suitcase down to the shore turns out to be trickier than one might imagine. Streets parallel to the coast tend to be reasonably flat, but the town is built on terraces rising steeply from the oceanfront. Some levels are joined by ridiculously steep roads, although there are also staircases for pedestrians to use as shortcuts. Either option requires careful managing of Cody's wheeled luggage, but he manages without losing control and watching it careen down to the next level. It helps that nobody else is out and about at this early hour.

I insist on waiting on the platform with him until his train starts loading passengers. "Tell me again what time you're landing at Dallas-Fort Worth?" We had looked over his new itinerary last night, but since his original direct flight wasn't available to rebook on such short notice, he has the flight schedule from hell, with stops in Newark and Chicago before finally arriving in Dallas.

"I'm not even sure what *day* I get home," he says with a deep sigh. "I think I'll just have time to shower and repack my bag, sleep a few hours, then head back to the airport to fly to Denver by Sunday afternoon, rent a car, and drive to Boulder for my first day of totally jet-lagged work the next morning."

That's going to be brutal. "Try to sleep on the overseas flight. You have that sleeping pill I gave you somewhere in your carryon?"

Normally I wouldn't share a prescription with anyone, but this seems like a necessary exception. Fortunately, my doctor ordered five pills for me when I asked for only two for my flights over and back.

Cody squeezes my hand. "I've got this, Mom. I got through a couple of all-nighters during college, cramming for finals, and aced my exams. Promise you won't stress out over what I'm doing and to just enjoy the rest of the walk. Just be chill."

Laughing, I lean into him and bump his shoulder. "Okay, Ace. I'll be chill." We lock eyes for a moment, recalling his dad's affectionate nickname for him.

"Ace," he repeats, smiling. "I haven't heard that since I was in high school."

We both turn as we hear a train gliding into the station. "Cody, I know you'll do great and I'm so happy you've found the sort of position you've been hoping for."

He stands and I rise to my feet reluctantly. This is it, then. He's really leaving and I'm really staying. Is it too late to change my mind?

He hugs me. "Bye, Mom. Have fun. Remember, you're a badass!"

I stand on my toes and stretch up to peck him on the cheek. "Safe travels, honey. It's been wonderful sharing my adventure with you. Now go create your own adventure. I love you."

"Love you too, Mom." And he's off. I walk down the platform, trying to spot him through the windows of the carriage, but with no success. Perhaps his reserved seat faces the opposite side. In almost no time, the train starts rolling and soon recedes from view.

As I trudge back uphill toward my lodging, I'm most certainly feeling sorry for myself. I miss Cody's company already. I miss Bryan more than ever. I'm determined not to start crying as I walk along these narrow roads in a country where I know no one and no one knows me. But suddenly a thought occurs to me and I blurt out, "I forgot the beans!" just as an elderly lady passes me headed the opposite way.

"What's that, love? *Beans*, did you say?"

Jolted out of my gray mood, I can't help but laugh. "I suppose I did. Don't mind me," I say, giggling like a schoolgirl. "Have a lovely day!"

As I scurry on, still chuckling, I hear her call after me that I should have a lovely day as well. What else can be said when one encounters a crazy American carrying on about beans?

I can't remember how our silly family joke began, but I'm sure Bryan was the instigator. When we'd make up our grocery shopping list, he'd make a point of checking that we had a good supply of canned black beans on hand, "Because you never know when you might need them!" If he left town for a conference, not only would he tuck a sweet note to me under my computer mouse or in my underwear drawer, but he would sometimes stick a can of black beans in the shower where the shampoo usually sat, or beneath my pillow. The more unexpected the discovery, the more delighted I'd be and the harder I would laugh.

Cody might discover black beans in his backpack at school or in his usual seat in the car, held in place with the seatbelt. "Daaaaaad!" he'd moan, but he found the game just as entertaining as I did. So, late yesterday afternoon, as Cody focused on booking a flight from Dallas to Denver and reserving a rental car, I headed out to buy a few items for my lunches along the next portion of my hike. When I spotted a small can of baked beans in the shop, I couldn't resist buying it and surreptitiously tucking it into his pack, which he had rearranged to use as his carryon for the flight home.

I meant to get him to discover the beans before he left St. Ives and share a laugh and a memory together. Will he be stopped by airport security for attempting to carry baked beans onto the plane? Maybe I'd better call him and confess what I've done. He could eat them as a second breakfast on the train and avoid an international incident.

Chapter 8

It feels great to be walking the South West Coast Path again. What with saying goodbye to Cody and then filling my rest day with tasks like doing laundry and scouring Colorado real estate and rental websites for affordable housing for Cody, I felt off-kilter and unsettled. I think Cody should have arrived home early this morning – that is, UK time. Which is around midnight where he is. Too confusing! I had hoped to hear from him once he landed in Dallas, but I'm sure he's totally frazzled after having changed planes twice and dealing with customs and coping with jet lag. There will probably be a message from him when I finish my walk today.

I resolve to clear my mind of everything but the trail and the wildflowers and the ocean and the rock formations. But I can't seem to ignore my apprehension about the tough section that must lie ahead. Will I be able to scramble up the enormous boulders Penelope described without Cody to give me a hand, or will I be forced to wait until another walker happens along to help me conquer the challenging parts?

As with previous hiking days, the trail varies as the hours pass. There are swampy sections which I must traverse using stepping stone paths that others have conveniently enhanced to make them less challenging. These lead to steeper, dryer slopes of gravel and on to flat expanses of low grasses and wildflowers. Overall, the route is steeper and far rockier than it has been, so I have to watch my footing more carefully so I don't trip. But none of it has presented anything I haven't encountered regularly when hiking in Colorado's mountains.

Approaching an inlet, I marvel at the lush ferns growing along a narrow stream. Even more remarkable are the two thick granite slabs spanning the water – a perfect bridge for walkers. The stones must be at least five feet long and two feet wide apiece, and are aligned perfectly to form a ten-foot span. How in the world did they move them to this spot? I haven't heard of anyone using mules to haul in the materials to build this trail. In fact, one hiker we spoke to several days ago noted that the trail crew must carry in everything they need, using that explanation to justify the insanely steep steps we've encountered along the way.

Sitting on a rock on the far side of the bridge is a woman wearing a vibrant blue shirt, her backpack resting beside her. Her salt-and-pepper hair is pulled back into a long ponytail. "Hello," she calls out as I approach. "Would you care for a blueberry scone? Unfortunately, I have no clotted cream nor jam."

Trying the traditional combination is on my to-eat-while-in-England list, but I gratefully accept the sweet biscuit even without the toppings. "That sounds *lovely*," I say, trying out a British-sounding phrase to fit the setting. When I take a bite, I try to imagine what it would taste like with the two sweet toppings. "Delicious. Thank you. Did you bake this yourself?"

She laughs. "I'm afraid mine wouldn't have traveled well from Australia. These are from a little shop I found in Hayle. I wish I had looked around for a proper bakery instead, but these travel well."

And here I had assumed she was British, but from a part of the country with a slightly different accent. We introduce ourselves – her name is Carolyn – and we chat for a bit about our experiences thus far on the Coast Path, and I learn that she's in England for two months, heading up north to hike another National Trail once she finishes walking from Hayle to Penzance, a slightly shorter walking itinerary than mine.

"That's ambitious, hiking all that by yourself. My plan was to be out here with my son the whole way, but he had to fly back early to the States."

"I enjoy traveling on my own, although I also fancy meeting others and spending a bit of time sharing the experiences," she says, tucking the remains of the package of scones into her pack. "My husband wasn't terribly keen about flying all this way to go walking, so he's off to climb Kosciuszko in the Snowy Mountains between Melbourne and Canberra, then over to Tasmania."

I stop myself from advising her to embrace as much time together with her husband as she possibly can, because you never know when that cherished opportunity might be taken away. But my life isn't hers, and it isn't my place to say such a thing. Swallowing hard, I silently give myself a little pep talk and vow to remain positive.

"Did you hear anything about the trickier part of The Path up ahead?" Carolyn asks. "My guidebook describes today as having a severe grade, strenuous, with scrambles over and around boulders."

Maybe our hostess in St. Ives wasn't exaggerating after all. "I've heard something similar. I hope I'm not going to need a boost in the steeper parts."

She rises and swings her pack back onto her shoulders, then laughs as we stand eye-to-eye. She may even be shorter than I am. “I was hoping you might be giving me a boost. Maybe we two wee ladies can forge on and somehow help each other through.”

With that, we march on together, sharing stories of other places we’ve hiked and places we’ve visited on vacation – or on holiday, as she puts it. We discover that we’ve both visited Vietnam, although about a decade apart. She and her husband have been to the western coast of the U.S., but she’d like to return and visit the four-corner states – Colorado, New Mexico, Arizona, and Utah. I report that Bryan and I visited New Zealand, but hadn’t gotten around to taking a trip to Australia. It was on our bucket list – a lineup that I’ll have to re-examine someday, when I can face that task.

Our trail is starting to turn even rockier than it has been thus far. We dance from one surface to the next, but neither of us is having any true difficulty with the terrain. In the lead, I reach a point where the way forward isn’t obvious, but I choose to turn slightly to the left and slip between two boulders that stand almost as tall as my head. With a slanted rock in front of me, I reach out and place one hand on the upper end, using it to steady myself as I angle through the gap. Looking back, I see that Carolyn has chosen a route that turns more to the right, but I’m comfortable with what I see ahead, so I stick with my plan.

After stepping up onto yet another slab, I advance forward and see that the surface slopes steeply and ends abruptly about a foot above the ground. Not fully trusting that I can keep my footing if I try walking down the rock ramp, I crouch and sit, then extend my legs in front of me to slide smoothly down the short distance on my butt, like a child on a playground. Moments later, I push myself back onto my feet, squeeze through a narrow gap between boulders, and discover that the trail is clearly visible once again. Carolyn hops down from a rock off to my right and strides over to meet me.

"How did your way go?" she asks. "Mine seemed pretty straightforward."

"Not bad at all. Kind of fun, really."

We continue along our path as it becomes smoother and easier to make good time. After consulting the map on my phone, I'm a bit puzzled. We're drawing close to my turnoff to head inland to Zennor, my destination for tonight. "You don't suppose that boulder section was the place where we'd be clawing our way through enormous rocks?" I had shared Penelope's description of the challenging obstacles, complete with an imitation of her frantic gestures.

We both gaze ahead, visually tracing the line of the Coast Path. My exit point is probably only 500 feet ahead of us. "Blimey, I think we aced it!" she says, grinning.

Carolyn's stop is still a bit ahead, so we hug and offer words of encouragement as I turn off the Coast Path to follow a narrow road into the tiny community of Zennor. With luck, we'll run into each other again in the days ahead.

Although there are a number of cars parked in a lot near the pub where I'll be staying tonight, it appears that there are very few businesses or even residences in this town. But the pub has Wi-Fi, so I check for messages from Cody. There's nothing new since his response to my confession of having sneaked the can of baked beans into his carryon – ***lol mom!!*** – followed by a string of *emojis*. How odd that he still hasn't sent anything since arriving home. On the other hand, his insane schedule still includes repacking for his flight from Dallas to Denver and heading back to the airport yet again. I can't imagine how he's holding up. I send him a quick text wishing him well and ask him to check in with me when he catches his breath.

After depositing my backpack in my room across from the pub, I decide to follow the signs leading to a small gift shop and a counter selling the local ice cream, called Moo-maid of Zennor. I had read that there is a famous legend of a mermaid attracted by the beautiful singing voice of a local man. They met and fell in love in the ancient church across the road from my room, then ran away together back to the sea, where their vocal duets can still be heard. The whimsical Moo-maid company logo features a cow with a fish tail. I text a photo of my scoop of chocolate ice cream to Cody – ***See what you're missing?*** Just a little nudge to remind him to text me back. The dairy, whose buildings seem to occupy the largest portion of Zennor, produces the creamiest ice cream I believe I've ever tasted. I don't think you can find anything fresher than having the dairy next door. Somehow I resist the temptation to order a second scoop of another scrumptious flavor.

Let's see. So far I've tried baked beans at breakfast (my pallet isn't quite ready at that hour), Marmite (the jury is still out), scones (plain), and Cornish ice cream (a winner). Still on my list: Cornish clotted cream and, of course, fish and chips. But tonight, I'm going with *Moules Marinières*, which the barkeep explained to me is mussels in a white wine sauce. My mouth is watering! I can find fish and chips in any village.

STOCKISTS OF
Moomaid
ICE CREAM
of Zennor
LEGENDARY
CORNISH ICE CREAM

Chapter 9

I can't decide if I'm annoyed or worried. When I awoke this morning, I fully expected a response from my son to my several messages, but there was nothing. Assuming he's trying to get back on a normal sleeping schedule, I wouldn't expect anything new from him for the next seven or eight hours, so I resolve to focus on enjoying today's walk. And I can only do that if I focus on my surroundings instead of my over-committed son thousands of miles away. I hope this new employer recognizes what a dedicated employee they're getting.

This morning is starting out overcast but bright. Although I don't expect my photos to be as stunning as the ones I've taken on sunny days, I still stop from time to time to try to capture the rugged configurations of rock formations hugging a cove far beneath me and the power of the ocean waves pounding the base of the cliffs. The winds along the promontory are strong and chilling today, in contrast to their gentler versions on sunny days, when I was sweating so profusely that the breeze felt like a cooling life saver. I take a break and settle onto some rocks close to the point of the headland, finding that the surrounding bushes shelter me from the wind as I sit and eat lunch. Looking back along my morning's route, I can see the trail roller-coasting past estuaries and inlets, snaking its way along the meandering coastline. I've been watching for Carolyn, but having no idea if she likes to start hiking earlier or later than I do, I'm starting to doubt that we'll meet up again today. Too bad – I enjoyed her company.

Crunching on bites of my tiny apple dipped in peanut butter, I don't realize immediately that the moisture I'm feeling on my hand isn't juice spraying from my apple. I scan the sky. It has become noticeable grayer and the drops are becoming more frequent. I take another big bite from my apple, scoop a blob of peanut butter into my mouth as a chaser, and stuff the food back inside my pack. I decide to don both my raincoat and rain pants. Even if it's a light rain, I want to keep myself and my clothes as dry as possible. Back home in Colorado, a thunderstorm can unleash torrential rain and drag the temperature down twenty or even thirty degrees in no time. I'm feeling a bit overdressed at the moment, even a bit overheated, but I prefer that to hypothermia.

Before I set off down the trail leading away from the tip of the high bluff, I wrap my pack in its own rain cover. Soon I hear a gentle patter of rain drops on my hood, which I've donned over the ball cap I was already wearing. Walking with my head lowered, I can see water accumulating on the cap's brim, then dripping in front of my face. Looking down at my feet as I step carefully on wet rocks in the track, I realize the bottoms of my pant leg have slipped beneath the heels of my boots.

Oh, the joys of being five foot two. I bought these rain pants especially for this trip, knowing that I'd need to roll up the legs several inches. Hemming them to fit my short legs would have been complicated, since they have a lovely feature of zippers that open all the way up the sides of the legs so they can be donned easily over boots and hiking pants. In the rain, they've unrolled and wrapped under the back of my shoes, which could be disastrous in slippery trail conditions. My boots provide traction, but I'm certain that my nylon rain pants will not.

I stop to lean against an ancient stone wall likely built to keep sheep or other livestock away from the cliffs. I pull on short gaiters that wrap around my ankles, tucking the muddy bottoms of my rain pants inside. With a strap that runs beneath my boot and an elastic band around my lower calf, the nylon gaiters should shield my lower legs from further sogginess.

The weather never develops into anything truly nasty, but the rain remains steady and the world turns gray and unappealing. I plod along through puddles and mud, and the route swings inland a bit, depriving me of even muted views of the shore. I long for a place to sit for a few minutes, but when I finally spot a bench, the rain increases and the idea of sitting in puddles on a bench looking at a colorless world has lost its appeal.

The Coast Path leads through a collection of buildings and equipment which were part of a tin mining operation here at one time. Or maybe they're still being used today – I'm feeling too chilly and miserable to recall what I once read in the guidebook about this area. My gloves are sopping wet and my hands are freezing. As I plod along, I debate going gloveless or digging out my warmer gloves from my pack. But that involves removing my pack and its cover, retrieving the warm gloves, removing the wet ones, finding a place for them, covering the pack again, putting it back on ... the list of steps involved seems like an impossible set of actions. So I do nothing. I simply slog forward, wondering how many miles I still have to go today.

What was I thinking? How did I ever imagine that I could walk all this way? Why didn't I return home early with Cody?

My feet ache. I'm cold. I'm tired. I long to take a break, but my desire to get this over with is even stronger. I plod on.

The trail crosses a small parking area – the first sign of any sort of a nearby human settlement that I've seen in hours. I contemplate calling for a cab. Although I have no idea how to describe this spot, I could provide GPS coordinates to the driver, which might or might not work. With my mind processing thoughts even more slowly than my feet are advancing me forward, I abandon the plan and just continue trudging along the Coast Path.

Is it still raining or are those tears leaking down my face? Both, I conclude. If Bryan were here, I'll bet he would have insisted on calling for a ride and...

If Bryan were here. Or if Cody hadn't gone home. If I weren't all alone.

Only when the village which is my stop for tonight finally comes into view do I realize that I haven't been eating or drinking anything since the deteriorating weather interrupted my lunch break. I know that I can become lethargic and out-of-sorts if I don't provide myself with enough "fuel" while hiking. My blood sugar is probably low, I'm dehydrated, and my body is begging for electrolytes. Noticing that there are hardly any drops of water forming on the bill of my ball cap and that the late afternoon seems brighter than it has for hours, I suck on my tube leading to a bladder filled with energy water and dig beneath my rain pants for the pocket in my hiking pants that holds a small packet of cookies from last night's B&B. I devour them.

"Almost there," I declare out loud, studying the directions on my phone. I realize that the rain has ended, other than a few stray drips now and then, so I flip back the hood of my raincoat.

"Thank goodness," I say, a genuine smile on my face. What a fool I've been today. I make a silent pledge to not let myself get into a funk again on this journey. While I might not have been thrilled with the weather, I could have avoided letting myself spiral downward like I did. Bryan was always there to help "take care" of me in situations like this. Well, I'm going to live up to my son's assessment of my strength. I need to do a better job of taking care of myself.

I can do this.

***

I drag my soggy body to my room and immediately check for heat coming from the radiator or the warming towel racks mounted in the bathroom, but both are cold. I fiddle with a dial on the heater and wait a minute, but nothing happens. Meanwhile, I fetch dry clothes from my suitcase – eternally grateful that the luggage transport service has come through once again! – and change out of my damp and dirty clothes in the bathroom. I toss my muddy rain pants and socks into the bathtub, planning to rinse them out later. Noting that the hems of my hiking pants are also wet and filthy, I toss them into the tub as well.

Feeling even more of a need to eat than to clean up, I don dry clothes and head to the on-site pub. Before taking my place at an empty table, I stop to ask the man who showed me to my room about the heat.

Glancing at his watch, he explains that the two heating devices in all the guest rooms are on a timer that will come on later this evening. "Is the room cold?" he asks, appearing quite puzzled, despite the chill in the air.

"A bit. I was walking in the rain all afternoon and feel a bit cool."

"Ah. Let me see if I can override the timer then."

"Much appreciated." I suppose I can understand his confusion – it's warm and cozy here by the bar. Plus, it seems that Brits are far more comfortable with cool temperatures than we Yanks are. Every hotel or guest house we've checked into has had its windows open wide, even when it was only in the 50s outside. That's 10 to 15 degrees Celsius, I remind myself, practicing the conversion in my head.

I log in to the pub's Wi-Fi and check for messages. No response to my text to Cody. I switch to emails, ignoring the daily list of deals on e-books, a Meet Up note about a hike this weekend, and the notification about my latest electric bill. Nothing there from my son either, but that was a long shot. Cody once told me that email is only for old people.

What's going on with him? My annoyance is hovering near desperation. I tap out a quick text – ***How's everything going? Are you in Colorado now? Please reply!*** – before setting my phone down and ordering my meal. *Chill*, I remind myself. That should be easy, since I've literally felt chilled for hours today.

By the time I return to my room, I feel alive again. I've eaten a delicious meal, the radiator is radiating, and the towels on the rack in the bathroom are toasty-warm. All I need now is a hot shower and to curl up in bed with my book. And to hear back from my son, who still hasn't responded to my messages.

Stay calm. Today is Sunday, so he's dealing with flying to Denver and driving to Boulder. I'm sure he'll respond when he gets settled in his hotel tonight. Which will be ... one or two in the morning here.

Nothing's going to happen before I retire for the night, so I'm letting go of being the hovering parent of a grown man.

As the hot water cascades over me in the shower, I'm relieved to realize that I'm once again feeling enthusiastic about the coming days of hiking. As long as I hear something from Cody.

I wake a few hours into the night and can't resist checking my phone. Still nothing from my son. *Give it a rest. He must be so jet-lagged and stressed out about starting his new job tomorrow that he's just forgotten to reply.*

Only that's not my Cody at all.

Chapter 10

When my phone rings at 3:00 A.M., I nearly fall out of bed trying to answer it. "Cody?" I choke out, my voice rough and hoarse from sleep.

"Hey, Mom. Sorry to wake you, but I just got all your messages."

My emotions exploding like fireworks in my brain, the next thing out of my mouth is, "I've been trying to reach you for *days*!" Realizing that I'm sort of screaming, I tamp it down a bit. "I know you've got a lot on your plate and had to make your travel and work stuff a high priority, but Cody, it's been *days*!" There I went again. *Chill. Stop yelling at him.*

"But Mom," he says, frustration in his tone, "Listen. I left my phone on the train to London. And I did send you messages. I had to borrow a friend's phone when I was in Dallas, then a guy in line at the car rental place in the Denver airport let me try sending you another message from there. I sent texts. Emails. I even called from the landline here in my hotel and left a message on your voicemail. I just got a cheap burner phone tonight and finally got my number ported over to it so I could check for messages. Like, literally minutes ago. That's why I called right away. I could tell you were getting worried."

I press my hand against my chest and focus on slowing my breathing and my racing heart. "I'm sorry I jumped down your throat. I should have known you wouldn't just forget to let me know you were back home safely."

We talk for a few minutes longer, postulating that my spam-blocker apps may have zapped his various messages because they came from unrecognized sources. "Sorry to hear about losing your phone. I'll bet that's added to your stress in taking care of all your travel arrangements. Plus, it wasn't cheap."

"I felt like someone had removed part of my brain. But there's good news too. I did a 'find my phone' search while I was waiting to board my flight out of Heathrow. Turns out it was at the lost-and-found at the train depot and I've made arrangements for them to ship it back to me right here at the hotel in Boulder. It should get here by Wednesday."

"That's great! How wonderful that someone turned it in."

"Yeah. Somehow I can't picture that happening in a big city in the U.S. So, I'm sure you need to get back to sleep, and I've got some manuals to get back to reading before I go into work tomorrow."

I wish him luck and apologize again for my earlier outburst.

"No problem, Mom. I understand and I love you, too."

I'm so lucky to have such a wonderful son. I collapse onto my bed and fall asleep again immediately.

***

My hand-rinsed clothes and damp boots finally dried out before I dressed to resume my walk this morning. I realize with astonishment that I'm excited about getting back on the Coast Path.

The sky is revealing pale blues and delicate white clouds and the verdant green fields I cross shimmer and sparkle until the moisture from yesterday vaporizes. The ocean displays a surprising range of colors as waves break against a pristine, untouched beach at the base of the cliffs I follow. Yesterday's washed-out grays and dreary mood have washed away.

I cross from one broad expanse of grass growing like perfect golf course greens through a gate only to encounter another wide field, this time featuring a grazing flock of sheep, their wool apparently spray-painted with a lovely shade of turquoise on their sides. Some also sport orange smudges toward the back of their bodies.

I snap a photo to send to Cody, planning to add a comment, ***Sheep graffiti?*** It must wash off when they do whatever it is they do to the wool after they shear the sheep. Or maybe this is the new thing. Instead of spinning wool into yarn and dying it, they just spray-paint the sheep and sell the fleece as is to anyone wanting a really warm cloak. That would eliminate lots of prep work. Chuckling to myself about my imaginative musings, I turn and finish crossing the sheep pasture to yet another gate or stile to cross into another field. I'll wager I've passed through an average of ten structures each day that are designed to allow humans to continue on, but stymie the livestock that I pass from time to time.

My trek takes me past a very rocky beach to a smooth, sandy one where I pause for an early lunch and watch numerous surfers in wet suits playing on the modest ocean waves. High clouds and a brisk breeze would certainly discourage me from being in the water today, but they seem undaunted. On my way again, the South West Coast Path swings out toward a promontory and I spot a Coast Guard building situated with a broad view of the sea. I descend an actual, normal staircase with mostly even, concrete steps and even a railing to a vantage point overlooking dramatic sea stacks.

I've been noticing that yesterday's dampness has really brought out the snails. I keep an eye out for where I step so I don't crush any on the trail. I follow the route as it climbs and swings out to yet another headland. I seem to be reentering civilization, as I spot buildings and find the Coast Path intersecting a paved driveway by a large building. Seeing that people have gathered at the end of the promontory, I circle around the structure and stroll along the edge of the graded viewing area, clearly demarcated with knee-high stones and furnished with telescopes and informational signs, and realize that I have arrived at Land's End, the westernmost point of Cornwall. I gaze at the ocean below, but since I've been enjoying that perspective for over a week, signs on the building draw my attention. *First and Last Refreshment House in England.* I suppose if you are arriving or departing by sea, this spot is the first or last business you'll encounter. But it's the *Cornish Ice Cream* sign that I can't resist. This seems like a fine spot to partake. The brand isn't Moo-maid, but it is equally scrumptious.

Delightfully refreshed, I carry on with my journey. Rounding another prominence, I see that the ocean has carved out many deep caves in the cliffs, sometimes digging all the way through to the other side, forming a natural arch above. The waves seem larger today, and there's more white froth on the water, which might explain the large number of surfers out playing.

As I've seen many days, there are dozens of untouched beaches far below me, as well as accessible ones. Crossing yet another prominence, I spot the world's largest orange cone, like the ones used to mark off a construction zone along a road, only this strange object is about twenty feet tall. All I can figure is that it's some sort of marker for ships to use to navigate. Or an extremely serious *no parking* zone.

Descending toward the next cove, I'm puzzled by what I'm seeing ahead. At first I thought there were two animals near the lowest point of the track. There is often a stream or estuary at these spots, so it would seem likely that animals might frequent an area like this. But as I draw nearer, I realize there are two people down on their hands and knees.

I stop a short distance before reaching the couple and it's clear that they are searching for something on the ground. The woman glances up and nods my way. "Lost a hearing aid, he has. One of those wee little ones that sits behind his ear."

The man sits back on his haunches with a groan. "I could have chosen red or blue, but I thought beige was best. Now the bloody thing blends in with the ground."

"Would a headlamp help?" I offer. When the man looks puzzled, I add, "A torch? Would that help?" feeling proud of knowing the British term for flashlight.

"Oh, a headlamp. Sorry, I didn't hear you clearly. Must be your accent."

His wife gives him an irked look. "Or your bad hearing." She smiles at me. "Yes, that might be a help. Thanks!"

Setting my backpack on the ground well away from the area they're searching, I pull out my rain gear, remembering that I keep emergency items stowed in the very bottom of the pack. I reach deep inside to feel around for the mesh sack I use for the headlamp, a small first aid kit, and the like. Wait – I'm feeling something completely unexpected as well.

A can of baked beans. I can't help but giggle, wondering how long ago Cody stashed it there. Have I been carrying it since the day I hid a can in his carryon? Even longer? Or did he find my little gift and transfer it over to my pack? How funny!

The couple have stopped their search and are looking at me like I'm nuts. "Sorry. I just discovered a practical joke from my son. Here," I say, retrieving the light and turning it on, "see if this helps."

It does. The hearing aid is recovered and placed in his pocket for safekeeping until he can clean it.

He thanks me, then she moves closer and speaks quietly. "It wasn't your accent, you know. It's actually quite easy to follow."

"Thank you." I'm sure that was meant as a compliment. I hadn't really thought of myself as having an accent, but now that she's mentioned it, I suppose it's all in your perspective, isn't it?

When I arrive at tonight's lodging in a charming little village bordering a stream flowing toward the ocean, my hostess shows me to my room, which is beautifully decorated, bright and inviting. Thus far, I've been pleased with every pub, hotel, and home-like B&B that I've stayed in. Like the others, the bed looks very inviting, with its puffy duvet to curl up under. Everything is immaculately clean, and this particular abode provides utterly enormous bath towels and the fluffiest, most luxurious bathrobes I think I've ever seen. Perhaps that's because I'll need to exit my bedroom into a hallway in this woman's home to reach the bathroom.

"No worries – you aren't sharing this bath with anyone else," she says as she shows me how to turn on the lights and the heated towel rack, one of my favorite amenities of all since I rinse out socks and underwear every evening. And I love the feel of a heated towel when I step out of the shower!

“Now, I do need to let you know about obtaining an evening meal. There really is nothing available here in our village.”

“What other options are there?” I ask. While pubs seem to be quite reasonably priced, I don’t mind trying a restaurant instead. Or even a simple place that only does fish and chips.

“There’s a lovely pub in the next village just a mile and a half up the road.”

She must see the dismayed look on my face. Once I arrive at my lodging, I’m in rest and relax mode. I just want to clean up, eat, and crash. Three miles round-trip sounds like nothing earlier in the day. Right now, it sounds like a death march.

“I can call a taxi for you, if you like. And phone ahead for a reservation.”

I love this woman.

Riding in a vehicle feels so odd after all the walking I’ve been doing. I passed the 100 mile mark today! I’ve made the right choice. The road is extremely narrow and dense hedges line both sides for a long stretch. There is absolutely zero shoulder, so no possible way for a pedestrian to step out of the lane of traffic. When we arrive at the pub after the very brief trip, the driver asks what time he should come pick me up again for the return ride.

“Half seven?” he suggests.

Seven-thirty? Looking at my watch, I decide I don’t need an hour and a half for dinner by myself. I’ve found pubs to be quite efficient in bringing out an order. “Let’s make it 7 o’clock,” I counter.

Dinner, as usual, is delicious. I decide to be adventurous and order a Fish Pie, and it is a delightful surprise. Beats the heck out of a frozen chicken pot pie filled with two tiny chunks of chicken and a few overcooked vegetables in a dense sauce.

The fish is plentiful, the vegetables roasted to perfection, and the crust is a treat of its own.

My waitress seems to fret over my eating alone, but I've become accustomed to it and actually enjoy focusing on my food. I don't linger long after I pay my tab, though, preferring to sit outside in the courtyard to wait for my ride.

The taxi pulls up right on the dot and I thank the driver as I climb in. Within minutes, he's whisked me back to my Bed and Breakfast.

"How much do I owe you?" I had looked for a meter on the dashboard to monitor how much the ride would be, but didn't spot one.

Without hesitation, he replies, "Thirty pounds."

I must have misunderstood. That would be close to forty dollars. He must have said thirteen pounds, which seems pricey for two five-minute rides, but perhaps there's a ten pound minimum.

"*Thirty* pounds?" I ask, enunciating carefully so he won't have difficulties understanding my American accent.

"Right. Thirty pounds."

Do I challenge him on this? Ask my lodging hostess if this is normal? I'm not being an Ugly American here, am I?

I decide to just let it go. Maybe he kept the meter running the entire time I was eating. How many fares could this man possible get each night in such tiny communities as these? My thirty pounds may be his entire income for the day. I pull out my credit card and he has me tap it on his card reader to complete the transaction.

In another life, I might have argued with him. I certainly would have rehashed the situation again and again, fretting all evening and possibly into the following days. Tonight, I'm choosing to just let it go.

Instead, I'm sending a selfie to Cody with me holding the can of baked beans. ***You got me!***

Chapter 11

It doesn't seem possible that I will have walked 118 miles by the end of today. This is it. My final leg of the trip, covering the last thirteen miles with over 2,000 feet of elevation gain. I'll spend two nights in Penzance, then head home.

Thinking back to the early days of planning for this journey, I remember my concerns about taking on more than I could handle. I asked myself: *Can I hike eleven or twelve miles in a day, with an average of 2,000 feet of gain per day?* Yes, if I train for it. *How about two days in a row?* Uh – probably. *Three days in a row? Four? Five?* Now I have serious doubts.

Still, we managed to talk ourselves into hiking for six days, taking a rest, then walking four more days, a rest, and a final push of five days to our original end point. Some of that decision was because we wanted to spend our rest days in larger communities where we might be able to do laundry, enjoy a bit of in-town sightseeing, stock up on supplies for lunch, and have more than one choice of restaurant. Thus our choices to rest in St. Ives and Penzance, and end in Falmouth. Cody and I eliminated that final five-day leg as requiring more time than he could take off.

And now, look at me! I'm about to finish this trek feeling strong. Over 100 miles! I even did part of it totally on my own, which I never would have considered before circumstances pushed me in this direction. Remarkably, I don't want this experience to end. I wish I could walk another 100 miles. But, of course, it's too late to make that happen.

Isn't it?

Wanting my final day on the South West Coast Path to be memorable, I force myself to shut off my internal thoughts about everything but what I'm doing right now. I look back at the coastline behind me, marveling at the fact that I've already visited every prominence I can see, fading into the far horizon. I spot an attractive structure that blends into the slope of the nearest rocky granite outcrop among the sea cliffs. My hostess last night told me about The Minack Theatre, an open-air venue with an ocean view to die for. What an experience it would be to watch a play in a setting like that!

The Coast Path descends and I enter a region where the trail becomes a bit rocky and I'm passing through a passageway bordered by tall bushes and knee-high flowers and grasses. The vegetation is so thick that I can barely see the trail squeezing its way through. When I emerge, I spot a waterfall plummeting into the sea and I stroll through a broad meadow filled with buttercups and tiny daisies. I hate to tramp on them, but there's no other option. The trail drops again and I'm in the midst of a thick grove of trees – a rarity right here on the coast. Within the shade of the small forest, flowers and ferns have gone crazy. This section more resembles a tropical forest than what I'd expect to see in this part of Great Britain.

Taking a short break in this verdant oasis, I look up as a pair of young men approach. "The University of Colorado – that's my alma mater!" I say as I spot the t-shirt one is wearing. The black shirt features the silhouette of a buffalo and the initials CU in gold, and the state name, Colorado, splashed across his chest just below the logo. He drops his head to peer down at his clothing.

"That's brilliant. You're here on holiday from Colorado, then?

"Yes, I am. Are you a student at CU?" I ask.

He laughs. "Not at all. I just took a fancy to the picture of the buffalo and Colorado seems like a place I'd like to travel to someday. See the Grand Canyon, and all."

Should I tell him? If he actually decides to travel to America, he might be disappointed if he finds that he's in the wrong place. "Actually, the Grand Canyon is in Arizona. The Colorado River flows through it, so it's easy to see why you made that connection. Colorado has lots of high mountains, so it's also well worth a visit."

The other guy chuckles and comments, "Good thing we got that all sorted. That would be a long way to go and not find the Grand Canyon! I hear it's quite immense. Hard to miss."

The CU guy joins in laughing at himself. I ask if I can take a photo of him and his logo shirt and he seems quite pleased to oblige.

They wish me a pleasant journey and take off at a fast clip along the trail. Small world, right?

A few hours later, I'm wondering if the town I've spotted far ahead might be Penzance. The distance seems about right and it's a considerably larger settlement than any I've passed through over these past two weeks. Checking my map and GPS, I'm certain that I'm only a mile or so away from my final destination.

Instead of forging ahead, I sit down on the sloping grasses and flowers beside the Coast Path. I don't want this to be over. When I think back on how I was feeling before this trip, it seems like I was barely treading water. I'd go through periods of immersing myself in my work, then suddenly find myself unable to focus on anything. Every time I thought about Bryan – and I'm talking dozens if not a hundred times a day – I'd feel like I'd just sunk underwater again. I was drowning.

But out here, and in my time with Cody, when my memories of Bryan surfaced, they finally started feeling like ... joy. Warmth. Love. Not that I haven't had my moments of sorrow during this journey, but those emotions seem to be stepping aside to allow the more positive ones to emerge.

It's not only that. As long as I can remember, I've had a running commentary going on in my brain. I review and rehash, practice what I might say in a situation, make mental lists of what things I need to accomplish this week. When's the last time I turned off that internal monologue and totally focused on what I was doing right then? Before this trip, I'd be hard pressed to answer that question.

I take a few deep, calming breaths and tell my mind to go silent. Gazing around me, I admire the cluster of bluebells hanging beside my arm. The breeze is creating waves of motion in the long grasses in the field behind me, a lovely parallel to the swells of the ocean before me. The white buildings of the town in the distance sit in brilliant contrast to the low, green hills beyond, and I spot two – no, make that three – boats heading into the bay that I'll be visiting in a short while.

It's a crazy idea and I'm not sure how I'll manage to arrange the logistics, but I've made up my mind. I'm going to continue walking the South West Coast Path beyond Penzance. I don't know how much farther I'll go, or where I'll stay, but I can begin working on those questions once I arrive at my lodging this afternoon.

And I have another wacky notion concerning Cody, but I'll need to run that one past him. I think it's brilliant, but he may think his mom's lost her marbles.

"Places to go, things to do, people to contact!" I declare as I get to my feet and stride energetically toward Penzance.

Chapter 12

"Long Horizons Walking Holidays. This is Penny. How may I help you?"

"Hi, Penny. This is Joni Walker and I'm currently on a walk on the South West Coast Path that you folks arranged."

"Oh yes, Mrs. Walker. I recognize your name."

"Please – call me Joni."

"Of course, Joni." I hear the tapping of a keyboard. "I see that you should have arrived at Penzance today. I hope your accommodations have been satisfactory on your journey."

"Every place has been excellent. In fact, I'm enjoying myself so much that I'm calling to see if I can extend my trip and go on to Falmouth, which was our original plan when we first booked in 2020." I realize that I've fallen back into plural mode – *our* plan, when *we* booked. Of course, at that time *we* were sending in our final payment for a joint vacation that had to wait because of restrictions on international travel.

"Very good! And when are you wishing to take up your walk again?"

Speaking with confidence in the hopes that making last moment lodging arrangements isn't an impossible task, I respond, "Since I already have lodging for tonight and tomorrow here in Penzance, ideally I'd like to re-book those five additional nights starting on Thursday."

There's a long pause before Penny speaks again. "I would love to tell you that there's no problem with obtaining bookings at your previous lodging selections, but on such short notice, I can't make any promises." There's a slight hint of panic in her voice, but she's handling this well.

"I'm sure I'll be happy with whatever accommodations you can find. I'm even open to changing which towns I stop in, if necessary, although I'd prefer keeping my daily mileage no more than...sixteen miles." *Did I really say sixteen?* Yes, because I'm a badass and my son will back me up on that.

I hear Penny letting out a sigh. Please don't tell me it can't be done! Although, if Long Horizons doesn't find any vacancies in their vetted list of B&Bs, I could always search for places myself and hope for the best. With any luck, I won't also need to find my own transport company to tote my suitcase from place to place.

"Joni, can you give us until tomorrow afternoon to see what we can accomplish?"

"Absolutely! Thank you so much for whatever you can do. And with such a short timeframe, please go ahead and reserve as many of those nights as you find available. I'm even willing to book two nights somewhere if that's their minimum stay. I have complete confidence in the places your company recommends."

We talk through a few more details and I acknowledge that my payment for our (my) original 2020 trip might not fully cover these new reservations, but the difference in cost from what we paid for initially shouldn't amount to much. Forge ahead!

The other aspect of my brilliant idea is something I need to run past Cody, since it affects him even more than it does me. When I return to my hotel after dinner at a nearby Thai restaurant, I decide that an email is the best choice for presenting my proposal to him. He's still in the middle of a workday there in Boulder, so I certainly can't interrupt with a phone call and I dislike sending lengthy text messages.

It takes me several edits, but I'm finally satisfied with what I've written. Reminding myself that he probably won't read it and respond until well after I retire for the night, I launch my missive into cyber space and sit back with a satisfied smile. Won't it be delightful if he accepts my plan! I know it's not without potential drawbacks, but overall it seems like everyone will come out ahead.

***

As I'd hoped, there's a reply from Cody waiting for me when I wake up.

Wow Mom. That's a really generous offer, but I need a little time to think about it. Love you.

That's the Cody I know. Doesn't like to jump into things without weighing all his options. Makes lists of pros and cons. When he told me about this new job offer and that he planned to jump on a plane and turn his whole world upside down to take it, I was flabbergasted. Then he shared more details about how he learned about the opening and the attractive offer they made him, and I realized he hadn't acted on impulse after all. Except for the part about covering up his screw-up on the starting date. He had been following a lead about the position for weeks before he landed an interview. When I expressed shock that he had given notice to his Dallas landlord and employer before his new appointment was finalized, he explained that he had two other irons in the fire in the Denver area and felt confident that at least one would come through for him. Fortunately, his top choice wanted him.

He has so much on his plate for the immediate future. This weekend he's returning to Dallas to pack up everything and haul it to Colorado, where he doesn't have a place to live yet. Rents are outrageous. I found only a handful of studios or one-bedroom apartments for under $1,000, and those looked pretty questionable. I didn't realize how fortunate Bryan and I were to have a low-interest mortgage payment on the house we bought years ago. My outlay is well below the cost of a dingy flat with a miniature refrigerator and a two-burner stove.

Which is why my proposal makes so much sense, at least from the money perspective. We split my mortgage payment. He ends up paying less than half of what he'd cough up elsewhere, my cost is cut in half, and he can move back out anytime. He'll have the bedroom and bath in the basement, plus plenty of room and privacy to set up a home office in the "rec room." The wet bar has a microwave and mini-fridge, but naturally he'll be welcome to use the well-equipped kitchen on the main floor. With the house sitting on a sloped property, there's even a separate entrance to his quarters in case he feels the need for privacy regarding his comings and goings, or people he may wish to entertain downstairs.

We already know we can live together in close quarters. How much closer could we have been, given some of our tiny accommodations here in Cornwall! We'll each have a reasonable amount of privacy in my house, especially since I'm determined to always remember that he's an adult now, not my little boy. I think it could work. Let's see if he agrees.

***

I fill my rest day by exploring Penzance on foot. I stroll along the waterfront, enjoying watching a wide assortment of boats and large ships out in the bay. One strikes me as having potential as a pirate ship, and I smile, recalling scenes from the musical production, *Pirates of Penzance*, which I streamed a few weeks before coming on this trip. Making my way through an older part of town, I stroll along Chapel Street and surrounding narrow, bustling roads, browsing through antique stores and bookshops, art galleries and gift shops, narrow hotels and inviting pubs, clothing shops and bakeries. All these quaint and very Cornish businesses interspersed with stores selling the latest electronic devices, medical supply companies, grocery stores, and banks. The intermingling of buildings dating back to the early 1800s with their stone facades beside those with a 21st century storefront fascinates me.

My path back to my hotel winds past old townhouse-style buildings where vines of lovely purple wisterias wrap their blossoms around windows and doors. An entire city block consists of a solid mass of three-story buildings with a repeating pattern of pointed rooflines over narrow dormers, distinguished from one another by variations in their tiny entry gardens, or brilliantly-painted front doors or decorations on their gables.

I feel as if I've never seen so many buildings and so many people before, even though Penzance is a tiny fraction of the size of Denver. This is such a different world from the one I've been living along the Coast Path. The change of mood is fascinating while it also helps confirm that I'm not ready to end my walking journey just yet.

Bryan would be proud of me.

***

They did it! Long Horizons managed to re-book a series of Bed & Breakfasts taking me from Penzance to Porthleven to Lizard and Coverack. A new entry on my itinerary is for lodging outside of Mawnan Smith, which involves a bit of a walk inland, but Penny assures me that the accommodation will provide an exceptional experience. Finally, on to my ultimate destination, Falmouth.

The other adjustment to my schedule was to relocate less than four miles farther along the South West Coast Path to a town called Marazion. The hotel I stayed at for nights one and two didn't have an opening for another night, but by adding one additional night to my itinerary, Long Horizons placed me in an ideal location to explore St. Michael's Mount, an island clearly visible from Penzance and all around the broad bay. With my new travel plan sorted out, I changed my flight reservation – happily retaining a direct flight to Denver – and arranged for my train trip back to London and Heathrow Airport.

With all the logistics covered, I set out this morning to circle eastward around part of Mount's Bay to my next destination. I'm walking on a boardwalk for much of the way, still close to civilization and train tracks and roads, but eventually the Coast Path meanders onto a beach. The going is slower on the soft surface, but it's a pleasure to focus on the sand and the sea and the island, which I can now see houses not only a castle at its summit, but numerous other buildings closer to its shoreline. I'm excited that the timing has worked out so that I can make a low-tide crossing to visit the island, walking an ancient brick causeway that links the island to the shore.

Once across, I follow a path uphill to tour the castle, a magnificent stone structure that offers gorgeous views across the bay to Marazion and farther away, Penzance. The rooms inside the fortress are lovely and match my imagination of what an elegant castle should look like. Thank goodness for digital cameras. I've probably taken a hundred photos! On my way back down, with this being the setting for the old fable, Jack the Giant Slayer, I take the time to locate evidence of the assassinated giant, a heart-shaped cobble along the walkway. Cody would have gotten such a kick out of this. During a period when a much larger boy was bullying him at school, Jack's tale was what he requested again and again at bedtime.

After exploring the island's village and shops, I make my way back to the mainland before the tide rises and I'd have to book a ferry ride. By the time I check into my lodging, I feel more beat than I usually do on a long walking day. It seems that my legs and feet prefer a brisk, lengthy hike to strolling and standing for long periods of time.

Logging into my hotel's Wi-Fi, I squeal like a little girl when I read Cody's message. I'm going to have a housemate! Maybe it'll only be for a short time while he gets himself settled into his new job and new life, but I'm thrilled that he'll be close by once again. We missed him so much when he moved away.

Sometimes I like to imagine telling Bryan about special things that have happened since he's been gone. *Look, sweetheart, our boy is back in Colorado. I'm doing a lot better now. Yes, I know you're proud of me.* I'm proud of myself, too.

After uploading a few photos from today to Facebook, I scroll through the comments on earlier posts. Both my friends Rose and Jenny are apparently following my journey regularly, as they each click 'like' on all my pictures. But the person who surprises me is Meg, someone Bryan and I used to see regularly on hikes, but hasn't been in our lives much for several years. I'm not even certain she knows that Bryan died. Meg has been asking questions about the distances I've hiked, the weather, the lodging. It sounds like she's interested in planning a trip here herself. I answer her inquiries, wondering if she's still single, or if she's involved with anyone. Is she considering a solo trip like mine has become, or does she have a hiking companion?

I should reach out to Meg when I return home. See if she'd like to get together for a hike. She was always a fun person to be around, and I can't remember how we drifted apart.

While I'm in this inspired mood to be more sociable, I call up a deleted email message from a Meet Up group that organizes hikes in the Denver area. I've been silently stalking them for months, noting where they're planning on going but never signing up for an outing. *I might not know anyone. I'm not sure I want to ride in a car with strangers a long way. Maybe I won't feel like being around people that day.* So many excuses. Scanning the list of upcoming trips, I find one that's a week after my new return date. Being late May, they're sticking with trails close to the city at lower elevations – there could still be plenty of snow up high. The drive isn't long, the mileage they'll cover sounds like a piece of cake, and it's an area I've always enjoyed. And if I don't know anyone, maybe I'll make a new friend or two.

I'm signing up.

Chapter 13

The sea cliffs don't seem as rocky now as they were in the early sections of my walk. They angle away at a gentle incline, permitting soil and vegetation to cover their upper reaches, blanketing them in lush grasses and brilliant wildflowers. The slopes around the trail are also smothered with blossoms as spring progresses, and I imagine myself strolling through a painter's pallet of colors and hues. Whites, blues, pinks, purples, oranges, yellows – all breathtaking. One broad meadow is so enveloped in bluebells that I stop in awe, turning slowly in a circle to try to take it all in.

Moving on to a high perch overlooking a lovely beach at Praa Sands, there is a gathering of stand-up paddle boarders – like a pod of dolphins – enjoying the gentle bobbing of the waters in the cove.

I arrive in Porthleven by early afternoon. It's a cute little village with vendor booths lining the small harbor. Boats, like abandoned toys, are scattered on the sand and rocks amidst puddles of sea water. After checking into my lodging – a delightful house with a breathtaking view of the ocean – I follow my hostess's recommendation and walk to a restaurant that had caught my eye as I hiked past earlier. I'm seated in an outdoor sun-room. A young couple with a baby are shown to the only other table in that area and we exchange polite *hellos*.

After a waitress takes orders from both parties, the young mother smiles my way and asks where I'm from.

"Colorado," I say, "in the United States. How about you? Do you live here in Porthleven?"

The baby squirms in her lap and gets handed off to Dad. "No," she says, "we're here on holiday. Just down for the weekend. We're from up north."

Her accent is a bit tricky to understand, but I'm able to fill in a few blanks and follow what she's saying. We continue making small talk while the young father entertains the little one. I tell her about hiking the Coast Path and her eyes light up. "Andrew and I walked the ... *something something* ... path before we had Nelson." She smiles at the baby who is attempting to escape his father's grasp and crawl across the table to his mother. "We went less than fifty kilometers, though, so nothing compared to what you've taken on!" Andrew hands the child back to her.

Then he speaks for the first time, beyond that initial *hello*. I'm not even certain he's speaking English, although he ends with, "... *innit*?" which I realize is a question aimed at me. *Isn't it*?

My mouth is probably hanging open as I attempt to parse what I've just heard. I fail completely, but embarrassed to admit that his accent has baffled me, I smile ever so slightly, hoping his comment was something positive, and nod, acknowledging agreement with whatever he said. I watch their faces for a reaction, and it seems that I picked an appropriate response. Thankfully, Andrew says no more as I turn the conversation to the baby – how old is Nelson? Is he trying to walk yet? I figure I can smile and nod no matter how little I understand of their answers.

Saved by the arrival of my meal, I wave gaily at little Nelson and turn to my food. They resume their own conversation and I don't even consider eavesdropping. It would be to no avail. By the time I'm walking back to my B&B, half of the boats have been liberated from their dry perches as the tide rises and water begins to fill the harbor.

In the morning, I circle around to the other side of the anchorage and soon find myself back on my beloved track. Today will be one of my longer outings, covering fourteen miles with around 2,500 feet of elevation gain. As with all the previous sections, the gains come in the form of long, steep ascents up heavily-vegetated slopes, similar descents, and the dreaded straight-up-the-hill, too-tall steps. Either they aren't building them quite so tall, or my technique has improved. That, and my strength.

One of the several promontories I'll be traversing today is known as The Lizard, the southernmost point of England. As I work my way to view new vistas atop each headland, I keep an eye out for any signs that indicate that I'm on that special spot, but I never discover one. Finally, I approach a pair of women who've been ahead of me for the past half hour, but have stopped to take a break.

"Is that The Lizard?" I ask, pointing across the next bay to a tongue of land stretching out into the ocean.

"No, love. I believe that's a spot just before Kynance Cove. The Lizard is a bit farther on."

Of course, I could have checked my GPS mapping app, but I'm practicing interacting with people, something I thought I'd forgotten how to do over this past year. "Where does the name come from?" I ask. "Is the land shaped like a lizard?"

She smiles. "There are a few theories on that. They suggest that old Cornish words describing this land sound a bit like the English word 'lizard.' There seem to be several candidates for the original name, such as *lys ardh* meaning high court or *lezou* for headland."

So, nothing like the collared lizards or sagebrush lizards we find back home. We all set out together along the open terrain, winding our way in a sinuous path paralleling the cliffs. We reach another high point and spot an attractive beach far below. More steps are probably in our near future.

Instinctively, we stay high and follow the track as it curves back toward the mainland, but the grooved surface fades away and we're surrounded by cliffs. "Did either of you see a sign for another way?" one woman asks. We shake our heads. She pulls a map out of the back of the other lady's pack and begins to study it, while I retrieve my phone and zoom in on our location. "I don't know," the woman says, squinting closely at her map. "There's not enough detail."

Fortunately, I'm not having that issue. "Actually, it looks like we need to backtrack almost to the high point. There must be another path that takes us down there," I say, pointing to several people walking along a path well below us.

The plan works. There's a short, steep descent that connects us to the lower trail which slopes downhill and deposits us just above the beach we spotted earlier. My companions decide to continue on from there, but I want to explore the sands at Kynance Cove, so I descend a staircase and practice my balance moves as I make my way across a deposit of rocks to the beach.

The tide must have rolled out recently, because the sand is wet and there are puddles all around. Beautiful rock outcroppings rise from the flat surface, dark and glistening. I discover a natural rock cave with a ceiling tall enough that I'm unable to touch it with my trekking pole held high overhead.

Narrow tunnels of stone entice me to slip through, following the example of other visitors equally enthralled with this remarkable spot. Emerging from the maze, I laugh as I watch a man standing in a shallow pool partially surrounded by walls of serpentine. He calls his dog and the lab darts full speed toward him, then leaps into the water, executing a perfect belly flop. The animal rockets to its feet, exits onto the wet sand, then races back in again, this time attempting to run across the water. The man is soaked, but can't stop laughing at his pet's antics.

What a delightful detour this turned out to be. Feeling refreshed, I continue on to visit The Lizard and then turn inland to locate my bed for tonight in the town by the same name.

Chapter 14

Whether it's because I've been partaking in too much ice cream and other dairy products, or if my little jar of natural peanut butter has gone bad, my digestive system wasn't very happy when I arose this morning. The peanut butter goes in the trash bin, I swallow some Pepto Bismol, opt for only brown toast, a banana, and tea for breakfast, and linger in my room and its attached bathroom until my gut seems to have settled down. If today's terrain is similar to what I've experienced already, there could be very long stretches before encountering any sort of public toilet, or any semblance of vegetation or rocks to move behind for an iota of privacy if I have to "do my thing" again along the way.

I'm fine for a while, but nature is calling and I see no place to go that isn't in full view of anyone walking the Coast Path for a few hundred yards in either direction. Gritting my teeth, I try to distract myself by focusing on the open meadows and the sparkling of the sun on the water. I increase my pace when I spot a small settlement ahead. Following the route as it drops down to a tiny harbor with an ancient stone building, I look around frantically, searching for any sign of a public toilet or a business that might let me use theirs, but only see a lone house with a small garden and a couple of folks sitting outside reading the paper and sipping mugs of coffee or tea.

"Do you know if there's a public toilet anywhere nearby?" I ask, trying not to sound panicked.

The woman sets down her paper and scans our surroundings. "I don't believe so. Perhaps there's something up the road," she says, pointing uphill along the only street, which climbs abruptly from the waterfront.

I moan. I should have just taken care of this out in the middle of a meadow. I don't think I can manage to climb that steep incline in my current condition.

"Oh dear," she says quietly. "Would you like to come inside and use the loo in the house? Please pardon the mess – we've been staying here on holiday and are just packing to leave in a few hours."

Thank you, thank you, thank you! I drop my pack onto the ground and follow her instructions on where to find the facilities. I love this woman.

When I set out again, there's a spring in my step. I think my crisis is over. Once again, I'm engulfed in my environment, delighted to spot a lovely, solitary foxglove in bloom – the first I've noticed on my journey. And look at that! A section of land juts out to sea and there's an enormous open tunnel formed beneath it. Surely the thin bridge of rock will collapse in the not too distant future and a tower of stone will be left standing out there, stranded, surrounded by water.

Farther along, I spot a pair of kayakers paddling in unison in the waters of a beautiful little cove far below me. What a delightful experience that must be, like a synchronized dance over the ocean.

Arriving at my destination, I'm pleased to see that I'll be staying at a house with an incredible view of the water. Numerous small boats bob about on gentle swells and a few hardy souls splash in the surf. It has been a lovely, mostly sunny day, but the temperatures have remained cool. Perfect for hiking, but too chilly in my opinion for swimming in the cold waters.

Although it's a bit early for dinner, I realize I'm famished. No wonder – I ate very little this morning for breakfast and had only crackers and a tiny apple for lunch, having discarded my suspect peanut butter. Perhaps it isn't wise to eat fried food after my earlier stomach issues, but the smells wafting from a little fish and chips shop convince me to satisfy my cravings there.

Their menu offers a surprising number of choices of what type of fish to order. Cod and haddock I recognize; skate and plaice are completely unfamiliar. For no particular reason, I select the haddock, then wait outside at a picnic table by the water until the pager they handed me starts flashing its lights.

Holy cow – or perhaps I should say holy haddock! The bag they hand me must weigh nearly five pounds. Did I just order a family-sized meal? If so, it was remarkably inexpensive. I remove a small cup of malt vinegar and another holding a slice of lemon from the sack, then use both hands to lift the main container and peek inside of it. There's a gigantic filet of battered fish lounging upon a bed of chips – or French fries as we Yanks say. They must have given me the chip production from at least two large potatoes.

Any concern that the shop has prioritized quantity over quality is quickly set aside once I take my first bite. Heavenly! I have to force myself to eat slowly to give each forkful time to cool enough not to scald my mouth. Halfway through the fish portion, I'm already getting full, but I can't resist treating myself to more, so I pull aside the coat of batter and savor the rest of the extraordinary haddock. Sadly, I end up discarding the equivalent of an extra-large order of fries because I can't manage another bite.

***

While I've been immersing myself in my daily hikes, poor Cody has been dealing with relocating his belongings from Dallas to my house in Denver. Thankfully, a buddy of his has a large pickup truck and the two of them plan to drive in a two-vehicle caravan. Cody already managed to sell some of his bulkier furniture – his old bed, an unmatched dresser and end table, and a couch he picked up from Goodwill – so they can cram his computer, desk, and work chair; his clothes and hiking equipment; and of course his portable pizza oven, smoothie maker, and air fryer into the vehicles. Who'd have ever guessed that my son would grow up to be a kitchen appliance junkie? After Cody flew back to Dallas, he and his pal packed up and plan to head out well before dawn to make the twelve-hour-plus drive today, which is Sunday. If he can get his new office set up in my basement quickly, tomorrow he'll be able to enjoy his first day of working for the new company remotely. If he runs into technical glitches, he may have to drive to the office in Boulder and spend a second week on-site.

Poor kid. I hope he finally gets to settle into a reasonable schedule. He must feel like he's spent almost every waking minute on a train or airplane or in a car since he left St. Ives. I couldn't manage what he's been through. I'm relieved that my offer of a place to live may have lightened his load slightly.

Morning arrives with the raucous cry of seagulls. I may be getting used to their disturbing sounds – I no longer search for a wailing baby or injured cat when I hear the birds. Cody sent a text during the night saying he and his friend Mason had arrived safely and already unloaded Mason's truck so he can head off to Rocky Mountain National Park in the morning.

Sleep. Eat. Walk. This has been my world for two weeks, and there's little else that requires my attention. Despite today's clouds and a cool breeze, I lose myself in my environment and in watching for trail signs. As I've seen before, the South West Coast Path has been diverted due to foundering cliffs. However, these must have been more extensive than others, because I'm directed a considerable distance inland, following country roads and even crossing through a farmer's field, where I hesitate until I spot another "SW Coast Path" sign letting me know I'm still going the right way. My phone's map isn't very useful, since the track pictured must run right along the dangerous cliffs that I'm supposed to be avoiding. Still, this new challenge feels like a fun adventure, marching from one marker to another and experiencing a remarkably different landscape, a mere quarter mile or so away from the shoreline I've been following.

Eventually the signs lead me back to the familiar coastal views and I'm back on track. When my stomach rumbles, I'm surprised to realize that I've walked nearly eight miles already. I would have guessed only three. No wonder I'm hungry for some lunch! With another village just ahead, I press on and am rewarded when I find a café beside the beach there. Hot food! Bring it on!

I skip the ice cream for dessert, just in case my peanut-butter-gone-bad theory was wrong.

How is it possible that I have just one more day of walking after today? I toy with the idea of extending my trip again, but I realize I need to return to the real world at some point. It's not like I have unlimited funds nor unlimited free time, not if I want to retain my current clients, one of whom has a sizeable job for me to tackle starting a week from today.

The Coast Path skips across two bodies of water today. The first involves a narrow estuary that may or may not be filled with water when I arrive. I'm still unclear on the tide tables, and it sounds like I may need to wade in knee-deep water to cross even at low tide. My instructions from Long Horizons explain that I can take a ferry across – sometimes. If I'm lucky.

Fortunately, there's an actual walking path to head inland to a paved road and bridge over the river, then a route to double back and meet up with the official Coast Path again. It adds less than two miles to my trek, which I don't mind in the least, glad to stretch out my penultimate hiking day.

It's an enjoyable detour through woods sheltering shade-loving ferns and a wide swath of dense leafy plants featuring flowers that seem to explode with white spheres of petals. After completing my journey around this water obstacle, the trail guides me back to the familiar coast, which continues to evolve to gentle slopes down to the sea with more greenery than I saw in the early portion of my journey.

The second body of water I need to cross is serviced by a reliable ferry from a well-defined dock. An older man is sitting on a bench when I arrive. In his lap is an open bag, and he pinches something from it and drops it onto the palm of his other hand, holding it out in front of him. Without hesitation, two small birds land on his fingers and peck at the offering. I watch without moving a muscle, not wanting to scare them away, but they only flutter to the back of the bench while he deposits a few more goodies onto his palm.

"Robins," he says, smiling my way. "They're quite tame."

They're considerably smaller than the American robins I'm used to. So adorable!

"Here for the ferry, are you?" he asks as the birds partake of another helping. "Just flip that sign around so the yellow is showing and he'll come right across for you."

That sounds so much more encouraging than the earlier *If you're lucky* crossing. Good thing – this Helford River seems to flow far inland with no obvious bridge crossing for many miles, according to my map. At this time in the afternoon, I'm no longer hoping to extend my walk beyond the sixteen miles it looks like will be my total today.

Scanning the water and the far shore, I search for what I expect to be a sizeable barge heading in my direction. Rows of sailboats are moored to buoys, and I also spot other small vessels in motion, but it isn't until I spot one motorboat angling directly toward my dock that I realize my ride is here. I'm the only passenger. In a pinch, I think the ferry operator might be able to squeeze eight people on board, but it would be tight. I pay the fare and he deposits me on the far shore in a matter of minutes.

It isn't a long walk from there to my hotel, but I'm ready to kick off my boots, stretch out on my bed for a bit, then enjoy a steamy shower before dinner. When I undress, I spot the first full-length mirror I've encountered during this trip and I'm surprised at what it reveals. I have a waistline again! Menopause seemed to have re-molded my body like a clay sculpture, transforming it to resemble a sack of potatoes. My weight was within the recommended range, but I wasn't pleased with how I looked. After nearly three weeks of strenuous daily activity, my curves have been revealed while my legs are as trim as they were in my teens, yet more muscular. Is this the body of a bikini model? Hardly. But in the mirror I see a strong, fit woman who appears healthy and confident. And, dare I say, even happy.

What do you think, Bryan? Pretty good, eh? I find myself blushing at my reflection as I remember that special sparkle he'd get in his eyes...

Chapter 15

Give it time.

That was the advice I heard and read again and again as the initial numbness following Bryan's death faded and I experienced periods where I could hardly function. Those dragged out to weeks when I tried to fill every moment with work and a deluge of mind-numbing tasks before reverting back into a stretch when I struggled to leave my bed.

Time has passed, and I give credit to that salve, but I believe this long walk, including the time I spent training for it, is what has finally lifted me out of that cycle and will enable me to start living my life again. Do I still grieve? Yes, of course. But when I think of Bryan now, it's often with a smile, not with the feeling that an overpowering weight is crushing me.

Is it the exercise, endorphins frolicking through my system and lifting my spirits? Is it the incredible, ever-changing scenery and the anticipation of what I'll see beyond the next rise or around the next curve? Is it the cheerfulness of the people I've encountered? I'll even consider crediting baked beans for breakfast!

Whatever the cause, I've rediscovered what contentment feels like. Joyous anticipation, a sense of accomplishment as I've wrapped up each day's walk, the delight of laughing again.

This is it. My final passage along what has become my beloved South West Coast Path. I focus even more carefully on everything I'm experiencing. The signs warning me away from blocked tracks leading too close to a public footpath which has foundered. A crow perched in a leafless tree, surveying the yellow-flowering gorse and splashes of other flowers below. Other-worldly plants covered in tiny purple blossoms and towering ten or twelve feet into the air. The lovely fragrance of a hedge of glossy green leaves and lilac-like blooms, the refreshing relief of a breeze cooling the sweat of my brow, the brilliance of the sea, and the patterns of the clouds.

There it is ahead – the town of Falmouth. The long beach is littered with seaweed at first, but farther along the sand is clear and I see people walking or sunning or playing in the water as gulls soar above the surf, searching for food. The city sits beside a wide bay and the final promontory I'll spot ahead of me on this trip. It is beyond my hotel and beyond the train station I'll be heading to in the morning, but since the famous Pendennis Castle resides there, I decide to check into my room, change into my sneakers, and walk on out there. After all, I've only walked 10 miles so far today!

Henry VIII didn't hold back when he ordered the fortress to be built to defend the coastline. I climb extremely steep spiral stairs to explore level after level, peering through openings that offer long views in all directions. There are hulking cannons housed within the imposing structure as well as weapons on the grounds. Whether in Tudor times or during World War II, this stronghold has been here to protect these shores for 500 years. Amazing!

With one final food item on my bucket list, I'm pleased to see that I can enjoy a proper Cornish

Cream Tea in a café in the building opposite the castle. To be honest, I'm not entirely sure what to expect, although I'm sure tea is involved and understand I'll also enjoy my first taste of clotted cream. Although the name conjures up something akin to sour cream, I soon learn that it more resembles whipped butter, but with a flavor akin to whipped cream. My order includes a personal pot of tea, a blueberry scone, and two small cups, one with the clotted cream and the other offering raspberry jam. Apparently there's a gentle controversy over whether to spread the jam and then the cream onto the scone, or if the cream goes on first. Choosing the diplomatic approach, I cut the scone in half and prepare it using both methods. I take a photo before sampling.

Conclusion: you can't go wrong either way. I text Cody, declaring ***We totally should have been ordering Cornish Cream Tea every chance we had!*** I need to research if clotted cream is available back home. Or learn how to make it. But I doubt it'll be the same.

Still not tired of walking, I explore a bit of the town, following the Coast Path signs through town and along busy streets. I spot a long sequence of row houses, each front wall painted a different pastel shade. Delightful! Finally, I can proceed no farther. I'm standing at the end of a dock where walkers who are continuing their trek would catch first one ferry across the wide waters to St. Mawes, then another to Place Creek to pick up the Path again.

Walk on, fellow adventurers! I leave you here.

Chapter 16

How often do we truly undergo a life-changing moment? For me, one of those moments actually spanned the three weeks I spent walking roughly 200 miles. Some details of the trip have faded from my memory during these past several months, but if I clear my mind, I can still retrieve the meditative calm and gentle euphoria I allowed myself to experience as my world focused on the simple goals. Sleep. Eat. Walk. Repeat.

Cody is thoroughly enjoying his work and we've found our rhythm in our shared home. We often eat dinner together, unless he has plans with friends. There's a wonderful lady in his life now, and I think things may be getting serious. Recently, Nichelle started joining Cody and me for our Wednesday movie-at-home night, and I'm delighting in getting to know her.

As for me, I'm still not a social butterfly, but I'm doing much better. My old friend Rose is recovering nicely from her knee surgery and we try to get out for a hike most weekends. We just try to avoid steep downhill sections, in deference to her new knee.

Kelli and Ellen, a newly-retired couple who attend and often organize many of the online hiking group's outings, are also extremely fond of hosting pot-luck dinners, and have invited me several times. The gatherings are small enough –no more than eight to ten people – that I never feel overwhelmed by meeting folks I don't know. Those evenings are quite entertaining, with serious conversations about life, the universe, and everything as well as hilarious, highly animated stories from Kelli about her many strange and even bizarre experiences while working as a hotel manager. Ellen, who seems quiet and introverted, turns out to have a quick wit and a talent for inventing puns.

It wasn't an easy walk, those 200 miles, and I still have the callouses on my feet to prove it. But it transported me from a dreary world where I felt stuck in the quicksand of grief to where I find myself today.

I've come home.

ABOUT THE AUTHOR

Photo credit: Debby Reed

Diane Winger is a self-described "retired software geek" who loves hiking, rock climbing, kayaking, camping, and cross-country skiing when she isn't glued in front of her computer writing, picking out books to add to her "to be read" list, and watching cat videos. She is a voracious reader who still gets goose bumps whenever someone introduces her as an author.

Diane is an enthusiastic volunteer in her community and is particularly passionate about literacy-related projects and organizations.

In addition to writing fiction, Diane has co-authored several guidebooks on outdoor recreation along with her husband, Charlie. They now live in western Colorado, but Diane was born and raised in Denver.

http://WingerBooks.com

Dear Reader,

I hope you enjoyed this novella. My own trek along a portion of the South West Coast Path in Cornwall was an experience I'll cherish always, and this is one way I've chosen to embrace those extraordinary times.

Perhaps this story brought back fond memories of one of your own adventures, whether walking the SWCP or enjoying some other special experience. Perhaps it inspires you to pursue a dream, whether it be to travel to a significant place or study a subject you've always been drawn to, or anything else that you find uplifting.

If that's the case, I'm thrilled that this story may have played a small role in inspiring you. Thank you for reading my book and for spending time with me.

Enjoy your journeys, wherever they may take you.

Diane

Books by Diane Winger

Faces

Duplicity

Rockfall

Memories & Secrets

The Daughters' Baggage

The Abandoned Girl

No Direction Home

Ellie Dwyer's Great Escape
(book 1 of the Ellie Dwyer series)

Ellie Dwyer's Big Mistake
(book 2 of the Ellie Dwyer series)

Ellie Dwyer's Change of Plans
(book 3 of the Ellie Dwyer series)

Ellie Dwyer's Startling Discovery
(book 4 of the Ellie Dwyer series)

The Long Path Home
Walking the South West Coast Path in Cornwall, England
(A Novella)

For more details, please visit Diane's author page on Amazon:
amazon.com/author/winger
or
amazon.co.uk/Diane-Winger/e/B002BRDGEM

Made in the USA
Columbia, SC
08 October 2022

69161305R00072